UNTIL THE ROAD ENDS

UNTIL THE ROAD ENDS

PHIL EARLE

ANDERSEN PRESS

First published in 2023 by
Andersen Press Limited
20 Vauxhall Bridge Road, London SW1V 2SA, UK
Vijverlaan 48, 3062 HL Rotterdam, Nederland
www.andersenpress.co.uk

2 4 6 8 10 9 7 5 3 1

British Library Cataloguing in Publication Data available.

ISBN 978 1 83913 316 9

Printed and bound in Great Britain by Clays Ltd, Elcograf S.p.A.

For my true and generous friend,
Dr Andrew Beck

1

It would be fair to say that Beau's life began one second before it almost ended.

He hadn't meant to stagger into the road, but he was hungry, starving in fact. The dustbins that lined Balham's alleyways had been mercilessly empty all week, leaving him light-headed and woozy, and his legs feeling like they were detached from the rest of his body.

This was why he tottered from the kerb onto the busy high street: why he found himself staring at the approaching lorry, hypnotised by the eyes of a huge metal monster, which roared and howled as it bore down on him.

He should have moved, he knew that. He'd survived on the streets for years so was adept at darting suddenly from danger, but this time, he didn't. Or couldn't.

The monster's lights held him, trance-like, drawing him deeper into their blinding depths. It blared a warning: a long, tuneless growl, but instead of galvanising Beau, it paralysed him.

He didn't want it to end like this. Of course he didn't. He wasn't old, or bitter. He didn't hate the world or the people who lived in it. But he *was* tired. Dog-tired. And his legs simply didn't understand either the gravity of the situation, or the simplicity of the order being sent by his brain.

So he continued to sit, glowing brighter with every passing moment. Neither cowering nor whimpering. He just watched as the lights enveloped him in an angelic hue, forcing his eyes to narrow and close.

But as he shut out the world one final time, he felt it shift, and then capsize, as two hands gripped his belly, wrenching him sideways, pulling the air clean out of him as the lorry roared one final disdainful roar.

Beau rolled, pulled tight into his saviour, and saw the landscape pirouette as they both dived for the safety of the gutter while the lorry tore by. What had just happened, he wondered, and whose hands were they, gripping him tightly still?

The dog tensed, trying to see who was holding him, but was clutched so closely to their chest that he could see nothing at all. He panicked. He didn't trust humans; he wanted to, but after all that had happened to him, he couldn't take the risk.

His entire body went rigid, but those hands held on. He bucked and writhed, expecting the human to become angry quickly, like they always had in the past. He waited for the hands to strike him, or the voice to shout, but neither came. Instead, his head was pulled into the nape of the human's neck, and a single finger gently scratched at a spot that had been troubling him for days.

If that wasn't enough to allow his tension to subside, there came a voice, not one of a grown human (who were always the worst, in his experience) but of a child.

'Steady on,' said the girl. 'Nuffin' to be scared of, is there? I got you, Beautiful. Just in time too, by the looks of it.'

Beau's legs stopped resisting all together, as the single finger became two, three then four, finding every itch and dry spot on his wiry back. Heaven.

The voice continued, singing softly in his ear. 'It's all right, Beautiful,' it repeated, 'it's all right.' And it was such a simple, heartfelt lullaby, that the dog relented, all fear and distrust forgotten. Within seconds, he was sound asleep.

2

The dog awoke in a living room. Modest. With a glowing fire, empty vases and an under-stuffed settee. There was an armchair with a thin man perched on it. Everything about the man was angular. His legs ran like drainpipes inside a pair of immaculately pressed trousers, his fingers sat like drumsticks, tapping anxiously on the arms of his seat. But as the dog's eyes opened, the man's face broke into a relieved smile so wide that it made him cough violently, and he was forced to push his thin, wire-rimmed glasses back up his narrow nose.

'Looks like someone is finally awake,' he declared, coughing again.

Instantly, four more pairs of eyes fell on the dog. The first belonged to a woman, as curvy as the man was thin, though the same kindness shone out of her. Her hair fell past her shoulders with a bounce, hiding the top of her flour-coated pinny. Judging by the smell wafting from the next room, she had been cooking some sort of pie and the smell alone rumbled the dog's starving belly.

The second pair of eyes belonged to a boy. He had volcano-red hair, plastered into a severe side parting, though three tufts stuck up at precise regular intervals, as if rusted stiff in an act of disobedience. He was slower to lean forward than the adults, but that may have been due to what was sitting on his lap: a cat; its build could only be described as hulking. The dog had met many such a tyrant, so wasn't surprised to see it wearing a scowl that declared, *You, Dog, are bad news.*

The starving mutt looked away, prompting the cat to hiss, which made its boy stroke it even more lovingly. The dog thought little of it, concentrating instead on the pleasure *he* was now feeling.

The fingers were on his back again. The same ones that had lulled him to sleep. They felt so good that he allowed himself to roll over, the owner of the fingers coming into view for the first time. All the dog could see at first was a smile. A smile that radiated the same warmth and delight as the thin man's.

'Ah, there you are, Beautiful,' the owner of the smile said.

The dog drank in the adulation. To a creature like him it felt alien, but wonderful. He looked beyond the smile to everything else around it: a befreckled nose and cheeks, dark brown eyes and matching hair pulled into loose, tired-looking pigtails. There appeared to be a dot of food stuck to her bottom lip, which the dog sought to tidy up with his tongue, making her giggle.

'You really shouldn't be calling it Beautiful, you know,' the boy said.

The dog's ear seemed to sag. Why? What had he done to the boy since waking up?

The girl, frowning, asked the boy the same thing.

'Well,' he replied, 'the dog's not yours, for starters, so it's not your place to be giving it a name like *Beautiful*. Plus, it's a boy . . .'

'How do you know?'

'Er . . .' the boy pointed between the dog's back legs. 'It's obvious, isn't it?'

It appeared that he was right.

'So,' he continued, 'Beautiful is a completely silly name. Especially when you see how ugly he is!'

That did not land well with the girl, who gasped and pulled the bedraggled dog into her arms again, as if shielding his ears from the insult.

'He is *not* ugly, Wilf,' she spat back. 'He's just clearly had a hard life. With a bath and a few good dinners, he'll be a champion. The best in show.'

The boy and perhaps the cat both chuckled at that.

'Unlikely,' the boy replied. 'But anyway, he's still not yours. And he'll always fall a long way short of being beautiful.'

The girl stroked the dog even more tenderly, fussing its ears in a way that left it totally disarmed.

'*You* might think so, but that's what I'm calling him, whether he's mine or not.' She stopped, and thought deeply before looking pleadingly at her parents with wide eyes. '*Beau*. I'll call him Beau. BECAUSE he is *literally* a long way short of *beautiful*. I think it suits him. Don't you, boy?'

Beau woofed twice. Once in agreement, and secondly at

the boy and his cat. The cat hissed back. The boy looked like he might do the same.

'Peggy,' her father said, his smile now tinged with concern. 'I'm not sure making the family any bigger at the moment is a good idea, are you?' He lifted the rolled-up newspaper from the seat beside him and Peggy knew exactly what he was referring to. The words *Hitler* and *Nazis* were written large everywhere.

'But Wilf has Mabel. What about *me*?'

It was a fair enough question. Anyone could see that Mabel was Wilf's cat.

Her mother and father shared a glance, and Peggy was unable to read its meaning; yet like most children in that situation, she knew that if she wanted her way, she would need to work harder for it.

'I mean, it really doesn't look like he has an owner, does it? He's got no collar, and *look* at him. If he does belong to someone, then they don't deserve to have him back. Not when they've treated him like this.'

Beau licked the girl's hand in appreciation. 'But if you want,' Peggy went on, 'I'll put up some posters. Tell people I've found him. That way, if they *are* sad about losing him, then they can do something about it.' She said it confidently, because to her mind there was no way anyone was coming for the dog. He'd clearly been living on the streets for too long for that to be a possibility.

The adults looked at each other again, then at the dog lying on their daughter and the obvious, instant adoration flowing between them. Her mother sighed in defeat.

'Sounds fair,' her father said. 'But if anyone *does* come forward, then Beau has to go. Agreed?'

'And if he doesn't remain the angel he is now, he goes then too,' her mother added.

'Of course!' Peggy said, her heart pounding with joy.

'Then we'll take it from there. First thing tomorrow, posters. Do you hear?'

Peggy nodded.

'Right. Supper. Leave Beau by the fire. Come on, Wilf.'

The family moved as one, Peggy closing the door after a final stroke of the dog's head.

Beau stretched out on the rug, closer to the fire. It didn't feel normal to him to be on the receiving end of such love, but it definitely felt good. Were these finally humans he could trust?

His eyes sagged, the flames warming him, inside and out. Sleep pulled at his edges and he began to surrender, until . . .

'Don't be making yourself too comfortable,' said a voice. 'And don't be getting any ideas, either. There's only one top dog around here. And that's me.'

3

Beau lifted his head, startled. His senses felt rather scrambled, pulled as he was from the verge of a safe, peaceful sleep.

His eyes moved quickly around the room, looking for the hound who had made the claim. He was most confused. There had been a lot to take in in the short time since arriving here, but he'd been certain there was no other dog lurking. At the same time, he knew what he'd heard, and so he clambered to his feet, nose pressed to the rug. If he couldn't see the intruder, he would definitely be able to sniff them out.

Beau's sense of smell was one of the main reasons he was still alive. He was quick too, certainly, and whip smart (you had to be to survive on the city's streets), but his nose had been his salvation on innumerable occasions. He could sniff out a meal in a bin from a hundred and fifty paces, and not just rotting slop that gave out an ungodly pong. He was talking about fine dining: a shard of pork crackling, a scrap from a shoulder of lamb, there was nothing his nostrils couldn't detect.

At that moment though, unusually, his mind wasn't on food. He felt confident after what he'd just witnessed that he would soon be fed, and fed well. Instead, he was in survival mode. If there was danger lurking somewhere behind the sofa, then he would soon sniff it out.

But Beau didn't find a thing. Well, that's not true, he smelled many things. Furniture wax and Brylcreem, daisy pollen and fountain pen ink, but no dog. He was certain of it.

'You really aren't the sharpest tool in the box, are you?' said the voice again, making Beau spin around to put whoever it was straight. But as he faced the armchair by the fire, there was no other dog, just the cat, Mabel, scowling disdainfully.

'Oh for pity's sake,' she said. 'Do pull yourself together. You *must* have known it was me warning you. No dog is *that* dense, surely?'

Beau didn't know how to respond. Not immediately. He knew of course that cats *spoke*. But he also knew that cats didn't speak to *dogs* unless they absolutely had to. To do so would be to lower themselves to the dog's level, and in cats' eyes, that would never, ever do. It was acceptable to tut or sigh when the idiotic mutts begged for a treat or rolled over for a belly rub, but *speak*?

'Sorry . . . was that . . . you?' Beau didn't want to sound like a dunce, but he had to be sure.

'Talking *at* you, yes,' the cat replied, with heavy emphasis on the second word. 'Don't think for one second I was talking *to* you. *That* would be a very different thing. And not something I'd countenance without an awful lot of forethought.'

Beau wasn't sure where this was going, or what it really meant, but didn't have to worry for long as Mabel went on.

'So I'll make this brief.' She spoke matter of factly and without once making eye contact, such was her arrogance. 'This is *my* house and *my* family. They may allow you to stay, of course, more fool them, but if they do, then none of those facts will change. I will put up with you, but will not fraternise with you. If they try to sit us together, by the fire or anywhere else, you will move. Not me. *You*. We are not friends. We aren't even acquaintances, so I'd suggest you accept that quickly. If you don't, then this cushy life that you think you've wormed your way into will be anything but. It will make the dustbin you previously lived in seem like the Ritz.'

Now Beau was used to meeting territorial animals. It was an everyday occurrence when you eked out an existence on the streets. But his experience was of sharp teeth rather than words, so this left him rather disarmed. So instead of heeding the feline words, he walked over to the sofa to try and thrash out some sort of peace, or at least a compromise.

It turned out, though, that Mabel was true to her word as, instead of continuing to lash out verbally, she now used her claws, swiping at Beau's muzzle, knocking him off balance, leaving him too close to the fire.

His blood boiled, not due to the flames, but at the indignity, and he curled his top lip in disgust, yellowed teeth bared for the first time. Mabel replied in turn, back arched, fur along her spine spiked like a porcupine, but as each of them prepared themselves for battle, the living room door eased open, and the boy, Wilf, strode in.

His cat, his innocent, saintly pet, was hidden by the back of the sofa, so all he could see was the rabid snarl of the dog on the hearth rug, and of course, he took great delight in loudly telling everyone exactly what he'd found.

'Mum! Dad!' he boomed over his shoulder. 'This stray . . . he's threatening Mabel! Come here, quickly.'

There was a clatter of feet, then a rasping cough as the mother and father arrived in the doorway, followed by Peggy, bursting in between them.

But what they found wasn't what Wilf or Mabel intended. Because if the cat thought she could outsmart Beau, then she was sadly mistaken. It didn't take a genius to realise that once the boy shouted, the others would come running. It didn't take a genius to realise either that if they found Beau with hackles raised, he would quickly find himself back on the street.

So by the time the family entered the living room, all they found was a dirty, straggly dog, blissfully asleep on the rug. In fact, if they listened carefully, they could hear the poor thing snoring.

'Wilfred,' his father exclaimed, after another phlegm-drenched cough. 'I don't know what your game is, sunshine, but we ain't falling for it. Any more lies about Beau and it will be *your* place in this house that's at risk, not his. Understand?'

The boy looked shamefaced, his cheeks flushing the same red as his hair. Mabel didn't look pleased either, and sulked against the sofa cushion. And Beau? He allowed himself a wry smile. The battlelines had been drawn, but he'd proved himself the cat's equal. And that deserved a long, warm and peaceful sleep.

4

Beau's life soon became as attractive as his name.

The family, the Alfords, loved him almost immediately. Well, most of them, barring the two obvious exceptions.

He didn't have to work hard to make Peggy and her parents feel that way. He didn't have to put on an act or trick them either; why would he, when warmth radiated out of them? Despite the rightful mistrust he felt for humans, he soon felt his guard being gently eased down.

These were good people. They didn't have a lot of everything, but what they had was shared, and appreciated. The house was warm, being mid-terrace, but it wasn't just about the heat coming out of the stove; it was the way they spoke and treated each other.

Beau had never heard so much laughter in his life, and not just polite chortles either. Big belly laughs caused by something on the wireless, or a joke the father had heard down the factory. Some were so riotous that the four of them would end up doubled over, roaring in delight. Beau joined in with his loudest, cheerful bark, even if he hadn't a clue why the punchline was funny. This only made them laugh even harder.

'I told you Beau was meant to be with us!' Peggy would roar. 'He has *exactly* the same funny bone.'

The only thing that ever seemed to stop them was when the laughter got too much for Mr Alford's brittle chest, and there would follow a hacking, endless cough echoing round the room.

'I'll get you some water,' Peggy would say as she dashed for the kitchen, leaving the man to try and smile from behind his handkerchief, his Brylcreemed hair collapsing in long strands across his face.

It would often take minutes for the coughing to end, though to Beau it seemed that the cure wasn't the water, but the love the girl showed. She'd stand at her father's shoulder, hand resting gently on him.

'It's all right, Dad,' she'd whisper. 'It will pass.'

The man would nod and reach into his lungs for air that wasn't there at first. But as she persisted and the man followed suit, he soon found small pockets that didn't have him rasping. Then, and only then, would Peggy move beside him, holding his hand gently, sweeping his hair back into place, until he looked smart enough to be photographed.

'There you go,' she'd say. 'Told you it would pass, didn't I?' And when it truly had, she'd perch gently on his lap, though it was hard to work out just who was consoling who.

From his spot by the fire, Beau would watch, taking it all in.

The girl was extraordinary. There seemed to be limitless amounts of compassion in her: Beau had found that on their first meeting. Yes, she had wrenched him from the road to save him from the lorry, but she'd done it with such care that he hadn't felt a thing.

But what he also learned quickly was that surrounding her soft centre was a tough exterior, one that stood her in excellent stead for the rigours of everyday life on their street.

When she wasn't at school or sleeping (Beau much preferred the latter: he quickly missed her whilst she was at her studies), Peggy spent her time playing outside, along with what felt like most of the children in the entire world. There were swathes of them, filing ant-like from every doorway, some of them clean and tidy, others looking as dishevelled as he had the day he'd arrived at the Alfords'.

The children filled every inch of the road and pavement, their voices shrieking and laughing simultaneously. It was chaos, pure and simple, and in the middle of it stood Peggy, playing every game on offer, like hopscotch and skipping with the girls, but never shying away from the boys' games of chase that often deteriorated into a lawless variant of rugby. It didn't matter how rough or ungainly the scrummaging became, Peggy would never stand down, even if she skinned a knee or took a rogue blow from an elbow. That didn't stop Beau sticking up for her, though, telling any young ruffian, regardless of his size, that he didn't like his girl being manhandled.

This always earned him an ear-ruffling from her that had him panting in joy, or even better, a scrap of food secreted into his mouth when he hid under the table at supper time. She certainly knew how to reward him.

He soon learned to play her games too. Standing guard was all well and good, but it all looked like so much fun. He tried his luck at skipping, and although nine times out of ten one of his legs became tangled in the rope, it was worth it for the delight the children expressed when he finally cleared it and sped to safety.

Hopscotch was less successful (one-legged balancing was beyond him no matter how hard he tried), but he truly found his sport with Hide and Seek.

He wasn't the largest hound, so hiding in original places was never a problem. The issue was that the children never thought to look for him. He was a dog, after all. No, where he excelled, every time, was in helping Peggy to hunt the others down when *she* was seeking.

He didn't cheat. When Peggy turned her back and started to count, so did he. He didn't need to sneak a peek as to where the others were hiding, because he could smell them. Every one of them, individually. Sometimes it was the suds used to scrub their clothes that he detected, other times, the blood on their grazed knees or the milk on their breath. He couldn't explain how he knew, he just ... *knew*, and while he never jumped the gun in tipping Peggy off (she had quite a nose herself), he took great delight in lingering near the hiding places of the most irritating boys who had claimed they would never be found by a mere girl.

Together, Beau and Peggy were quite a team. They were separated only during school hours, when Beau would wait impatiently on the front step until he smelled her imminent return. Then, and only then, would he dash the length of Boundaries Road, yipping at such a decibel you would think he had spotted a rabbit. Bounding into her arms, his delight was only matched by hers, and on the short walk home, Peggy would tell Beau about her day in such glorious detail that he felt as though he'd shared it with her.

5

Although Beau and Peggy's love for each other was clear and undiluted, there was also a shadow looming: not just over them, but the whole of Europe too.

This shadow was marching angrily and noisily, as the world watched, towards Poland. Reports had people glued nervously to their wirelesses: some sighed in resignation, others bit at their nails as they remembered the last time war had come knocking. Children were often sent to their rooms to do something more productive while the adults listened to updates and reports of the advancing Nazi army. In the Alford house though, the only thing stopping the children hearing the truth was the contents of their father's lungs, but Peggy knew he wasn't coughing on purpose. Long days in the factory, where smoke belched and swirled, did little to ease his asthma, and even after he'd spent twenty minutes under a tea towel, breathing in a menthol balm, he still spent most evenings barking far more than Beau.

'I'm trying to listen, Dad!' Wilf protested, a tin soldier in each hand, momentarily separated from their regiment, who stood to attention on the rug.

'Be quiet, Wilf,' snapped Peggy, batting at him with a firm hand. 'You know he can't help it.' The same hand generously passed Dad his cup of tea, though his shaking fingers threatened to spill it before it reached his mouth. 'Besides, nothing's changed since yesterday, has it? Hitler's still potty, in't he? You don't need to hear the wireless to know that.'

Wilf started to protest by pointing at his toys, moaning something about not being able to fight his own war if he didn't know the latest movements elsewhere.

To Beau, it didn't make sense. Hitler was a new name to him, there were no wirelesses in the alleyways of Balham and Tooting, but at the same time he knew the man was trouble. He could smell it in the room whenever his name was mentioned, see the creases set into Mr Alford's brow well after his coughing fit ended.

'It's a worry, of course it is,' he told the children, as Mrs Alford squeezed his shoulder gently. 'Hitler is not a nice man, and he's a persuasive one too. Those rallies he held: huge, they were, by all accounts. Filled entire city centres, and he's used films and songs to brainwash people.'

Wilf's eyes opened wide as his grip on his soldiers seemed to falter.

'But for every bad man like Hitler, well, there are a dozen men, twenty even, ready to stand up to him. He can make all the noise he wants, and march as far as he wants. But he won't get his way, not in the end. Not if everyone stands together.'

Mrs Alford smiled, but had clearly had her fill of war talk.

'And not if everyone's eaten their supper either. Hitler's

got no answer to the hidden powers of green cabbage, everyone knows that. So come on, into the kitchen, the lot of you.'

They did as they were told, Beau too (though Mabel remained on the windowsill, pretending to sleep). With the customary scraping of chairs on the tiled floor, the family sat, with Beau taking prime place beneath the table, knowing if he hid there long enough, he'd be fed scraps, whether it was intentionally (courtesy of Peggy's generosity) or otherwise (Wilf's lack of forkmanship).

He thought his masterplan was faultless, until Mrs Alford ferreted him out.

'Come on, you cheeky blighter,' she chided, shooing him towards the back door. 'I ain't daft. You'll be fed once we're done. Not before. Now get in that yard and wait your turn.'

She didn't mean it harshly, Beau knew that. Knew also that his bowl would be filled before the washing up was finished. There'd be scraps, and the inevitable slop of overcooked cabbage, but inside, there'd be hidden gems of beef or a sliver of ham. Worth waiting for.

Obediently, he padded into the backyard, hearing the door swing closed behind him.

It was a warm evening, clear and bright, which allowed the cries of street games to drift effortlessly. There was something strangely calming, almost percussive about it, and finding the last, shrinking spot of sunlight against the back wall, Beau lay down, contemplating a nap.

How lucky am I? he thought to himself. *How much and how quickly things can change.*

He'd never really known what true rest was when he lived amongst the bins of South London. If he could've slept with one eye open, he would have. But here? There was no need. His girl was a mere door away, her family too: even the cat wasn't a threat, not right now. So after one long and deeply satisfying stretch, Beau invited sleep in, ignoring a new sound that fluttered at the edge of his consciousness. It sounded like the *whup* of air being beaten incredibly quickly, but as it offered no obvious threat, Beau ignored it, keeping his eyes closed.

'Sleeping on the job, are we?' a voice cooed.

Beau opened one eye suspiciously, wondering if the interruption was the start of a dream.

'Up here,' the voice said, unhelpfully. 'Next door.'

Beau lifted his chin to the yard on his left, where he spotted a pigeon, strutting the length of its coop's roof. It may have been the early evening light, but there seemed to be a glow enveloping the bird, giving it an almost angelic quality. That could have been something to do with the energy of its movements, the lightness of its pacing, the way its chest puffed proudly in front of it.

'I didn't mean to wake you,' it said, without breaking stride. 'Though from the look on your face I clearly did. Sorry about that.'

'Not to worry,' Beau replied. It was hard not to be impressed by the bird, such was its verve.

'Family not need guarding tonight?' the pigeon went on.

'Having their tea. Don't think there's anything too dangerous in the stew. Just beef, though her cabbage *can* be deadly, the length of time she cooks it for.'

'Well, I'm sure it'll be in your bowl in no time. Though eating too much meat makes you sluggish. Slows you down.'

'Well, it's clear you don't eat a lot of it.' The pigeon was still sashaying the length of the roof, with no evidence whatsoever of tiring. 'I'm Beau,' he added.

'Bomber,' the pigeon replied. 'Not my idea. I fancied being called Spitfire myself, what with it being the king of the skies, but my brothers wouldn't have that, would they? Said it would give me a big head, a name like that.'

Beau nodded contemplatively. He could see what they meant, though the bird clearly wasn't lacking confidence anyway.

'So why Bomber?'

Bomber stopped parading for the first time. Didn't look sure he wanted to divulge the truth.

'I mean,' Beau went on. 'It's not a bad name, is it? Bombers are fast, stealthy, deadly!'

That seemed to make Bomber feel more at ease, his chest puffing out to an almost unnatural angle.

'Yep, you're right. Reckon I'm the same. I could give this Hitler fella a run for his money. Or so my brothers reckon. Depends what I've eaten. Though I have upset a good few pedestrians in my time. I don't mean to land it on them. But, you know, when you've got to go, you've got to go! Bomber by name, bomber by nature.'

Beau didn't really want to think about that and so he changed the subject.

'What do you know about this Hitler? I hear his name all the time from my girl Peggy's folks.'

'I know he's trouble,' Bomber replied. 'Whipping up a lot of people in his country into a frenzy. Filling up their heads about what's rightfully theirs, places they should take back, spreading hate. Won't be happy till he's running the entire world, that one.'

'Do you think he's coming over here?' Beau couldn't help but look at the sky.

'If he gets his way,' Bomber replied. 'Him indoors is always talking to us about it. Telling us our time is coming again.'

Beau was confused. 'What d'you mean?'

'Don't you know nothing about us pigeons? About what we did in the last war?'

'Er . . . should I?'

'Played a *massive* part, we did, practically turned the tide when things were looking grim. Delivered messages all over Europe. Vital ones, written in code. Without us, we'd be living in a very different world.'

'Would we really?'

'Too right, we would. That's why him indoors has us in training. Says it won't be long till the Ministry of Defence is knocking on his door, asking for his best birds with the strongest engines.' Again, the chest puffed out like an opera singer.

'Blimey,' replied Beau. 'And you're ready, are you?'

'I was born ready,' Bomber replied. 'But it never does any harm to look after yourself, does it? Take today, released us down in Brighton, he did, and we had to find our way back. Not far really, fifty miles, give or take.'

'How many?!' Beau replied, stunned.

'That's nothing. Did it without breaking sweat. Could've done it ten times over and, as you can see, I'm the first back. As always. So when the government do call, well, I'll be at the front of the queue, won't I? I'll be a soldier. Just like them before me.'

This was all news to Beau, but it was hard not to be impressed. Impressed and also a little scared, because if Bomber was to be believed, then the skies were about to become very busy, and very dangerous indeed.

6

As the weeks passed, it became more and more likely that Bomber was going to have his wish fulfilled. War with Germany seemed almost inevitable. Peggy and Beau saw it and heard it wherever they went: fear and anger, and sights that chilled them deeply.

Clusters of barrage balloons appeared in the skies, tethered to lorries by thick wires. At first, Beau feared they were German bombers, only feeling marginally safer when he heard Mr Alford putting Peggy and Wilf at ease.

'Clever beggars, our RAF. They know, you see, that a lot of the Luftwaffe planes have to dive before they can let their bombs go.' He pointed to the sky with a wry smile. 'Try and do that in the dark, then they won't see the wires. Let's see how well their planes fly when their wings have been sliced off.'

This may have brought a grin to Wilf's face, but not to Peggy's or Beau's. Without wings, without the ability to fly, those planes would fall as quickly from the sky as the bombs themselves. And they had to land somewhere, doing who-knew-what kind of damage. It wasn't something either of them wanted to contemplate.

Changes happened for the children too. Gas masks were

handed out at school, each one stored in its own small box, which Peggy and Wilf carried round their necks. Whilst Beau wasn't easily spooked (hardened as he was by his early years), he took great fright when his girl first appeared in the kitchen, face obscured by a mask that seemed to have a snout where her nose and mouth should sit. It took several minutes of calm voices and a good few treats to tempt poor Beau out from the pantry.

Time spent sitting round the wireless became more challenging too. *Children's Hour* was a blessed relief from the news bulletins that talked endlessly of advancing German troops and heightening tensions. Sometimes the news was difficult to understand, but both Peggy and Beau could tell that none of it was good, and they huddled together on the rug, glad of the warmth they offered each other.

It was in the yard, as the family sat inside eating, that Beau learned even more about the changes that war would bring. Bomber made sure of it.

'Gas masks won't be the last of it for the children, you do know that, don't you?' he said, strutting after another long flight home, from Eastbourne this time.

'Why?' replied Beau. 'What have you heard?'

'You wouldn't believe half the things I pick up as I fly home, so I'll just tell you the stuff that will affect you and your girl. All I'll say is, make the most of her while you can.'

'What does that mean?' Beau didn't like the sound of it one bit.

'*Evacuation.* Government thinks that as soon as war's declared, London's going to become a prime bombing target. So the little ones are going to be shipped off to the countryside to keep them safe.'

'But how will they do that? There must be millions of children they'll have to pack off.'

'No idea,' said Bomber, bristling slightly. 'I only hear these things when I stop for a rest. Sit on the right windowsills and you can learn what you need pretty quickly. So, take it from me, a couple of weeks from now, there will be hardly any children left round here.'

'I don't think it will apply to Peggy and Wilf. Their family's so close. They won't agree to be separated.'

'The government can be pretty persuasive when they want to be. And besides, try and put yourself in the parents' shoes: would *you* want your children here if bombs are going to be raining down every night?'

Beau knew the answer to that, of course he did, but at the same time, he didn't want to be anywhere but by Peggy's side. She'd saved him, gifted him this new, wonderful life. It was his duty now to keep her safe, but how could he do that if she was hundreds of miles away?

'Maybe they'll send animals with them?' Beau said, hopefully. 'I mean, if it's not safe for children, then it's not safe for us either, is it?'

Bomber didn't have time to reply however, as a new voice entered the conversation.

'Your naivety is laughable, dog.'

Beau turned to see Mabel stalking along the wall, the usual smirk on her face.

But if Beau was irritated by her presence, Bomber was downright scared, taking to the skies with a nervousness that he'd never previously shown. It wasn't until he was nestled in a suitably high branch that he looked or felt safe.

'Who asked your opinion?' Beau sighed, though he knew this wouldn't be enough to silence the cat.

'Well, honestly, listening to you two talk so naively, it's hilarious, it really is. You,' she spat at Beau, 'are as bright as *he* is brave. Do you honestly think anyone will really care what happens to us?'

'Peggy and Wilf will.'

'But they're children, you fool. And who listens to children? Not the government, that's for sure.'

'Their parents, then.'

'Have you listened to what is coming out of your mouth? Hitler is coming. Even if it's not in person, his planes are coming, and they will keep coming, and coming, until there's very little of any of this place left. The children's parents, and any other parents for that matter, are going to be thinking about one thing – survival. Their own. Not ours.'

'Then we'll run away, follow the children wherever they send them.'

'And who'll feed us? And keep us warm? Have you thought about that, genius?'

Beau hadn't. Of course he hadn't. All he knew was that the thought of being separated from Peggy made his heart hurt. If he was going to come up with a solution to the problem, then he was going to need time. Time, though, as it turned out, was one thing he did not have.

7

Everything happened so fast.

At first, there was good news, for some.

'There's a matter we need to talk about,' Mr Alford said, as he switched off the wireless. No one was upset to see him do that after what they'd just heard. Mrs Alford nodded in encouragement.

'It's clear that the next few ... well, months ... are going to be difficult. As much as we might wish it otherwise, war is coming.'

Peggy took a deep breath. Beau hopped up on the sofa next to her, paw on her lap comfortingly.

'Does this mean you're going to be a soldier, Dad?' Wilf asked. The boy had been obsessed with his toy infantrymen for years, but suddenly, the grip on his favourite didn't seem so tight. There was a glint of fear in his eyes.

'Well, that's the thing,' said Dad, with a cough. But it wasn't his normal cough, this one seemed designed to cover his emotions rather than clear his chest. 'Everyone is going to have to do their duty: men, women, children, everyone. And so yes, I thought it was only right that I join up.'

Beau heard Peggy sob once, her hand at her mouth, failing to stifle it. Her eyes glistened with tears, but she refused to blink for fear of setting them free. Beau nestled in even closer to her side.

'But when I went for my medical,' Dad went on, 'I was told that I'm not fit to serve. That my asthma is so bad I wouldn't last an hour in uniform. So I wanted to tell you that, together. And well, I hope you're not ashamed of me.'

But there was no shame, or judgement: there was only relief and tears and a stampede from his two children and his wife to hold him and tell him that they could never, ever think that of him.

They stood in the middle of the rug, in a scrum, with Beau circling them protectively. Even Mabel didn't seem to be wearing her traditional scowl (though she also had not moved from the sofa).

'Dad, this isn't awful news. And it doesn't make you bad or useless.' Peggy always seemed to know the right thing to say. 'It just means you won't be on the front line. It means we can all be together still, doesn't it?'

The scrum separated, and Mr and Mrs Alford sat the children down again. Beau leaped back by Peggy's side, scampering over a tutting Wilf to reach her.

'That's just it, Peg. I'll still have a job to do. I'm going to be an air raid warden. On the streets, keeping people safe when the bombs *do* start to fall.'

'*If* they do?' Peggy insisted, but Dad shook his head firmly.

'*When* Peggy, *when*. You've seen what's going on around you. The balloons, the shelters being dug. It's coming, and when it does, *none* of us know what it will be like. Not really. And so none of us know just how dangerous it's really going to be. That's why . . .' and Mr Alford coughed again, bending double when it didn't pass quickly, allowing his wife to step in.

'Which is why your dad and I have decided that the right thing to do is to have you evacuated.'

Peggy and Wilf's jaws dropped, but Beau's didn't. It was exactly as Bomber had predicted.

'But I don't want to go away,' wailed Wilf, instantly clinging to Mum's apron. 'And neither does Peggy.'

'Now, now, Wilf. None of us want this,' Mrs Alford replied. 'I didn't carry you both for nine months just to give you away to complete strangers.'

Beau held his breath and looked to Mum. Did this mean she'd changed her mind?

Mrs Alford didn't torture him any longer. 'Which is why we've spoken to your aunt Sylvie.'

Peggy's expression turned into a grimace.

'Aunt Sylvie?' Wilf moaned.

'That's right, Dad's sister. Aunt Sylvie.'

'But she doesn't even like us.'

Mr Alford coughed even louder.

'That's not true,' said Mum. 'She just doesn't have any children of her own, so she doesn't understand you like we do.'

'She doesn't have any children because she hates them!' wailed Wilf.

'If she hated children, then why would she open her door

33

to you? She may seem strict, and yes, she may be a stickler for the rules, but she's a decent woman. And think about it, she lives right next door to a lighthouse. How exciting will that be? You'll be safe there. And there's the beach to play on, whenever you wish. Imagine that?'

'But the summer is nearly over,' Wilf moaned. 'And the beach is rubbish in the winter. It's cold and windy, and the sea will be full of sharks and polar bears.'

Mrs Alford sighed. 'Wilf, there are many things I could correct you on there, but as you've never even been to the beach, I'll let it go this time.' She looked imploringly at Peggy as if for support.

Peggy sighed and searched for something, *anything* positive she could offer.

'It'll be fine,' she told him. 'And think about Mabel too. There's so many fields down there, it'll be mouse heaven for her.' The last bit was made up. She'd never even been to Aunt Sylvie's, but she had a vivid and unappealing sense of what it would probably be like. She didn't want to lie, she was no more thrilled than Wilf, but as the eldest, she felt a duty to lead the way. Plus, Beau *would* like the beach. He'd love it, in fact.

'Ah,' said Dad, returning to the conversation. 'You see, that's the thing.' The colour of his face suggested another coughing spree was moments away. 'The pets . . . well, Aunt Sylvie can't take them as well.'

At that point, Peggy felt no pressure to conform. 'She *what*?'

'She hasn't the space, Peggy, nor the money to feed them, either. There's not a huge amount of work down there, and she only just gets by as it is.'

'But we can't go without the animals! We can't!'

'I know it's not ideal, but—'

'But nothing, Dad. You've said it yourself. The bombs are going to be raining down, every night probably. And it's going to scare poor Beau witless without me.'

'And Mabel without me,' added Wilf.

But if the children thought this conversation couldn't deteriorate further, they were wrong, as Dad turned to fetch something from the dresser.

'Honestly, Peggy,' said Mrs Alford. 'We know how dangerous it's going to be here, especially for the animals. Everyone knows, even the government, which is why they've sent this to every house.'

And with that, Mr Alford produced a small, beige booklet.

'Air Raid Precautions for Animals,' read Peggy out loud from the cover.

She stared at the booklet, then at her parents' crumpled faces. Then, unprompted, she pulled Beau into her. And she had no intention of letting go.

8

This booklet was bad news. Peggy could tell that from the way it made her dad frown so gravely.

'What *is* it?' she asked, though as soon as she'd spoken, she wanted to cover her ears. 'I don't have to read it, do I?'

'Absolutely not,' Mr Alford replied. 'There are things in here you don't need to see.' He looked distraught, so much so that Beau jumped to the floor to offer him some moral support: that and the fact that he *did* want to see what was inside. If it were going to affect him, then he felt he had the right to know. He circled Mr Alford until he found the right vantage point. He was holding the book loosely, as if his fingers would become contaminated by clutching it too tightly, and as a result it had fallen open. What Beau saw took his breath away, as there, at the top of one of the pages, was an illustration of a horned cow, with a rifle's cross hairs trained smack-bang in the centre of its forehead. To make it worse, underneath there was a drawing of a sheep with the sights pointing clearly at the top of its skull.

Beau whimpered in fear and dread, a noise so distressed that it shocked everyone in the room. Mr Alford dropped to his knees with a cough to see what the problem was, but Beau was already on the move. He didn't want to be anywhere near the book, and burrowed himself deep into Peggy's side.

'What does it say, Dad? Please,' she begged.

'The government are worried, Peg. Firstly that there won't be enough food for everyone when the war starts, never mind the pets. And also that if the bombings start like they think they will, it will be noisy and scary, and most importantly, it will be too dangerous for them.'

'Even more reason for them to come to Aunt Sylvie's!'

'I'm afraid that can't happen. We've tried, Mum and me both, but your aunt doesn't have the space, Peg. And it'd be too much for her. Despite how good they both are.'

'But the government can't just leave the pets to be scared.'

'They're not suggesting that.'

'Then what *are* they suggesting?'

Mr Alford sighed deeply and looked to his wife. Reluctantly, she made to speak, but he stopped her, and kneeled before his children, one of their hands in each of his.

'I know this will be hard to hear, because we don't like it either, but what the government are suggesting, is having animals put to sleep.'

A frown crossed Wilf's face. 'What, until the war is over? But how will they do that, and how will they wake them up again? How will the animals know it's safe enough?'

Wilf was not an angelic child, far from it, but there was such innocence to his questions that Mr Alford had to steady himself before he continued.

'When I say *sleep*, that's not exactly what I mean, son . . .'

'What he means,' Peggy interjected, 'is that he wants to

have Beau and Mabel put down. Killed. Dead. That's what you mean, isn't it?'

She pulled her hand from his, not believing that those words could've come from her own father's mouth. This was the man who caught spiders temporarily in jars instead of squashing them, the man who only weeks before had taken Beau in, instead of casting him adrift back onto the streets. What had happened to him, to everyone, to think that this could ever be right?

Beau saw fear in Peggy's eyes, such fear that as she jumped up, he did too, back arched and teeth bared. But then he saw Mr Alford's face. Saw him merely mirroring Peggy's distress. Beau didn't know what to do or who to protect, but when Peggy decided her only option was to dash from the room, he did the same, following her all the way to her bedroom. Upstairs was usually out of bounds, but not tonight. The girl who had saved him now needed him. And nothing would stop him.

Peggy prowled the room, her tears both angry and distressed. Beau followed behind her, nuzzling her shins if she stopped for long enough.

'It ain't fair, Beau, it ain't. It ain't fair or proper or nothing. And I'm not going to let it happen. If they think I'll let . . .'

She stopped, drew a juddering breath, then smiled as Beau offered her his paw.

'Why don't me and you go on the run, boy? Show the adults they don't always know what's right?'

Beau sat extra tall, a single bark telling her he was onboard.

'We'll find a barn, or a farm, somewhere they love animals.'

Beau barked again. Anything she said.

But as the idea took shape and Peggy's hopes lifted, there came a knock at the door.

A slow solemn knock.

Beau and Peggy both held their breaths.

9

Never in her life had Peggy been scared to see her own father.

'It's only me,' he said, a deflated look on his face when he saw both his daughter and her dog cower. 'Come on, I'm hardly Hitler now, am I?'

Peggy didn't crack a smile.

'Look,' he said. 'I didn't mean to upset you. Neither of us did. It's a lot for *all* of us to take on board.'

'But you were alive for the last war, weren't you?'

Dad smiled weakly, like it was something he wasn't proud of. 'I was, but I was a small boy, weren't I? And besides, it was different then. Lads marched away to fight in the trenches. It was fought on the ground mostly. There wasn't the threat of bombers every night, like now.'

Peggy concentrated on stroking Beau.

'Me and your mum, we're just trying to do the right thing. The best thing. For everyone.'

'That's not true, Dad.'

'It is, Peg.'

'It's not. The best thing, the right thing, would be for Beau and Mabel to come with me and Wilf.'

'But I've told you, your aunt Sylvie can't manage it.'

'Then I'm not going either.' She tried to say it calmly, knowing that if she laced it with the anger she really felt then she'd just look petulant. 'I know he's not been with us long, Dad, but Beau's one of us, isn't he? Part of our family?'

'He is.'

'Like me?'

'Yes of course.'

'And would you put a rifle to *my* head?'

'No, but—'

'But that's just it, Dad. There can't be a *but*. He either is or he isn't. For me, he is. And if you and Mum feel different, then, well maybe it's a good thing I'm being evacuated, cos this ain't the family I thought it was.'

Mr Alford said nothing, but Beau saw him slump a little, like someone had placed an enormous weight across his shoulders. He exhaled loudly, stifling the inevitable cough.

'I can't promise you I can keep him alive,' he said, without looking up.

'I know you can't, Dad.'

'And I can't have my eye on him twenty-four hours a day either. I'll be busy, warden duties and all that.'

'You'll be important, as well as busy,' she gushed. 'But you know, Beau's bright. Maybe he can actually help you.'

'I don't have any doubt about that. Even if all he does is remind us of you, that will be more than enough.'

'Then you'll ignore the government? You'll keep him alive?' She was on the edge of the bed now, Beau too.

'I'll do my best. For him *and* Mabel. You know that.'

Peggy burst from the bed and into her father's arms. She held him so firmly and felt his decency so clearly that she couldn't envisage ever letting him go, and so for a good minute she didn't stop thanking him again and again as Beau circled them, barking his obvious approval, leaping against their calves in the hope of joining in. His great adventure was about to start, but he had no idea how long and perilous the road would turn out to be.

10

The suitcase at the door gave Beau hope. It was so small that Peggy would be home within days, surely. Then she walked reluctantly down the stairs, and Beau knew otherwise. She was dressed in her Sunday best, shoes buffed to a heavenly sheen and topped with a flat, woollen hat that Beau had never seen before. She moved stiffly, without comfort: she didn't look like Beau's girl any more. War was ageing her already.

Her eyes were narrowed and red, cheeks flushed, bruised almost, from her weeping. Beau whimpered and dashed to her side, knowing she would pick him up so he could tidy up her tears.

'Peggy, love,' Mrs Alford scolded gently. 'You'll cover your clothes in Beau's hair. What will Aunt Sylvie think if you arrive like a bag of rags?'

'That I don't want to be there,' she replied. 'And she'd be right.'

She regretted saying it as soon as it was past her lips. She knew the sacrifices her parents were making: in being without her and Wilf, in keeping the pets alive despite not just the government's disapproval, but some of the neighbours' too.

There had been comments as they'd walked down the streets, about their selfishness, about people going without food just so mere animals could line their stomachs. But the Alfords had replied with a dignity that made both Peggy and Beau proud.

'They're family, aren't they?' they'd said to anyone with the temerity to question their principles. 'And there'll be enough death round here without us adding to it.'

Sometimes that shut people up, sometimes it didn't, but the family had more on their minds than keeping face: the time had come to say goodbye to the children, and no one knew for how long. It made for a tense and emotional household. Even Mabel had broken her routine of long daytime naps to be present at the front door, curling herself around Wilf's calves as he clumsily swung his gas mask box onto his shoulder.

'Now, Wilfred,' Mrs Alford stammered tearily. 'You'll remember the two most important words for Aunt Sylvie, won't you?'

'Sweets and chocolate,' he replied cheekily.

Mr Alford raised an eyebrow.

'Oh, and *please* and *thank you.*'

'Good boy,' Mrs Alford sobbed, pulling him close, breathing in the smell of him, desperate to keep her youngest child close in any way she could. 'And we'll be down to see you if we can. As long as it's safe.' She left her lipstick on his forehead, whilst Wilf, unaware of the indignity, turned his attentions to Mabel, picking her up as she purred gently against his cheek. For once, she didn't look too keen about it, which surprised Beau. 'I wish I could hide you,' Wilf whispered too

44

loudly in her ear. 'Aunt Sylvie would never know.' Which was Mr Alford's cue to gently wrestle Mabel from his arms, which aggravated the cat still further, writhing and squirming before extending her claws towards his shirtsleeves. He'd had that happen to him on enough occasions to know it was time to drop her to the floor, which he did, allowing her to slink away to the corner of the room.

While this was going on, Peggy was bidding farewell to her mother. 'Make us proud down there,' Mum was saying. 'And keep studying hard. You're a bright girl. You might be a hundred miles away but schooling is still important. Don't neglect it.'

'I'd imagine Aunt Sylvie will be stricter than you,' Peggy replied, full of woe.

'True. And she's keen on the Bible's teachings, so please respect that. Don't be pulling faces or making a fuss, do you hear?'

Peggy's brain said one thing, but fortunately, her mouth replied another, which earned her a smile instead of a rebuke.

'And don't be growing up without me, either. You promise? I don't want you to come back a young woman. Not yet.'

That wasn't something Peggy could promise, so after one final, sob-laden embrace, her mother pulled away, comforted by her husband.

'Right then,' he said, reaching for his jacket. 'The train won't wait just because we want it to. And anyway, it's a long way to Tipperary.' He tried to smile, hoping they would too. They were always singing that song together.

But not today. There was no singing, nor swinging on their parents' arms. Instead, Mr Alford opened the front door and shepherded his wife, children and Beau out onto the street, where they were greeted by a long, cumbersome crocodile of children winding their way down Boundaries Road towards the railway station. They seemed to be dressed identically, a sea of grey and brown wools, their gas mask boxes bumping against them as they struggled gamely with their cases.

Adults stood on their front steps; some waved, others dabbed tearfully at their eyes with handkerchiefs, but this wasn't what Beau noticed. What he noticed was the lack of animals anywhere to be seen. Normally, there would be the sound of a dog greeting another, or a cat rifling through the bins. But today, the only other animal in sight was a still-sulking Mabel, who had sneaked outside.

At the station, Peggy moved away from her parents and dropped to her knees beside Beau.

'I don't want to go, boy,' she wept. 'Not without you.'

Beau whimpered his own agreement, pushing his muzzle to her chest.

'But I need you to be good, do you hear me? Look after Mum, look after Dad, and don't let Mabel rule the roost.'

Beau didn't need telling that.

'Most of all, stay away from trouble. Use that nose of yours in the best way you can.'

Beau snuggled in, pushing deeply against her.

'I need you at the end of all this, Beau. Do you understand? And I'll be waiting. Always.'

Beau whimpered softly, then felt Mr Alford's hands gently around his collar. He resisted. As did Peggy.

'And I'll write to you, do you hear me?' She tussled the long hair on his muzzle. 'Tell you everything that's going on. I know you can't read it, but Mum or Dad, they can. You will read my letters to him, won't you?' she implored.

'Of course, my love,' replied Mum through dewy eyes. 'Every word.'

'Then I'll write every week, without fail.' And she breathed him in, one final time, before Dad's hands moved from Beau's shoulders to hers.

'Come on, Peg, Wilf, we have to go now. The train won't wait if we're late. And you don't want to upset Aunt Sylvie, do you?'

At that moment, neither Peggy nor Beau gave a fig about Aunt Sylvie, and it took several more attempts for Mr Alford to separate them.

When he did, he handed Peggy and Wilf their luggage, before telling his wife he'd be back in the morning, adding quietly, 'You'd best keep a hand on Beau, just till we're out of sight.'

Beau felt Mrs Alford attach a lead to his collar, then felt it strain as his girl took her first slow strides away from him. He wanted more than anything to follow her, to keep her safe just as she had him, but he was just a mongrel, and Mrs Alford was stronger than she looked.

All he could do, as Peggy slipped away from him was cry: a howl as piercing and heart-breaking as any siren that would follow.

11

Peggy's absence filled Beau's world.

No sticks were thrown, no titbits were dropped, gone were the hugs and the scratching of his back, and most importantly, whenever he looked up, his horizon was empty. There was no sign of his girl leaning over him with her warm smile that melted his heart.

It hurt him, deeply, in a way that he hadn't realised was possible.

'I'm cross with myself,' he told Bomber one day, as he sat forlornly in the backyard. The pigeon had just returned from a training flight (he was the first one back, of course), and was strutting the length of the wall to show he still had plenty of fuel left in the tank. 'I mean, I've been on my own practically all my life. Slept alone, woke alone, never had anyone to feed or stroke me before, so why does this feel so . . . I don't know, hard?'

Bomber had the answer, of course. 'That's what them humans do. Make you soft. Blunt your edges, with their cooing and caring. No good for a soldier, that's for sure.' He plumped his feathers, making himself appear almost muscular. 'That's why I have as little to do with them as possible. I'll take their food, granted, let them put me in the basket before we get on the train, but that's it. No pet names, no cuddles. No good for a soldier to be soft. 'Specially not these days.'

'You heard anything yet about whether the army are going to need you?' Beau asked. It felt good to be thinking of something other than his Peggy.

'Not as yet, but war's only just really been declared. All I can do is look after myself in the meantime, keep the mind and body active, ready for the call up. Looks like you could do with following the same advice.'

Beau felt slightly affronted. Granted, his fur was a little more matted than usual, but without Peggy, who was there to look good for? He doubted he looked *that* shabby though. He thought it more likely that Bomber was judging him by his own lofty military standards.

His mind drifted to how Peggy used to brush him before she'd left. She always knew how hard to do it without ever causing him discomfort. She'd tease the biggest knots loose with her fingers first before starting with the brush. Beau let out an involuntary whimper.

'Oh dear. Is Diddums still feeling sorry for himself?'

It was Mabel, appearing as usual at the most inappropriate moment. She sat on the wall opposite Bomber, one eye seemingly on him whilst the other mocked Beau. Her ability to throw her attention in two directions at once was always a great irritation to him.

'Leave me alone,' he sighed, whilst trying not to look quite so broken.

'But it's so much fun ridiculing you,' she replied. 'And let's face it, it's the only reason I *do* talk to you. Without me, you'd be even lonelier.'

'Or maybe *you* would,' Beau said sharply.

'I don't know what you mean?'

'Oh, I think you do. I've seen you, scratching at Wilf's bedroom door to get in. The way you sleep on his pillow every chance you get.'

The cat looked momentarily sheepish. Which was quite an achievement. 'It's the comfiest, quietest spot in the whole house. Especially now he's not there. Why wouldn't I sleep there?'

'You *sleep* there, for the same reason I try and sleep on Peggy's bed. You sleep there because you miss him. And because it makes you feel safe. Admit it.'

But Mabel would not. Of course she wouldn't. Instead, she arched her back, revealed her claws and released a venomous hiss.

'I told you,' Bomber chipped in. 'Humans make you soft. The pair of you.' Though he looked a little soft himself when Mabel leaped in anger towards him, and he flapped his way to the highest point of his coop.

Ironically, this was the closest thing to war that the three of them came to for months on end. The only thing that fell from the sky at night was rain, and this did little for Beau's mood: in fact it made Peggy's absence feel even more unjust. His only contact with her was the letters she sent home, and he was made to work hard to hear them, despite them being written for his ears.

Mr and Mrs Alford would tear them open as soon as they arrived, their eyes scanning the lines hungrily, but Beau quickly became irritated when they failed to read them aloud for his benefit. He was a good dog, a patient one, who recognised that they *were* Peggy's parents after all, so he'd give them time, but if they tried to put the letter away after reading, he soon made his presence and feelings known, rebuking them with a sharp bark.

'What?' Mr Alford asked Beau, the first time.

'He wants to hear what Mabel said,' replied his wife.

'I'm not reading to the dog,' he said, blushing. He could feel a cough coming on.

'We did promise. And you've read it after all, it's as much to Beau as it is to us. More so, I reckon.'

So, after pushing down his embarrassment and sitting on the sofa, Mr Alford began, whilst Beau sat next to him, peering over his shoulder, looking to the rest of the world like he was following the words as he read them.

The letters were not easy to listen to though, especially the early ones. Peggy was lonely, and homesick.

It is so very different living by the sea, Beau. I'm sure when the summer comes it will be different, but at the moment, it's windy all the time. And cold. Wilf complains about it, says it's like living underneath a windmill, but that just upsets Aunt Sylvie.

She's a good person, I can see that now, and she works really hard. She looks after the lighthouse keeper at Anvil Point, cleans and cooks and washes for him. Her bread pudding is nearly as good as Mum's and she says she hates cabbage and never makes us eat it. But when we get homesick she doesn't find it easy to cheer us up. She can't find the right words like Mum and Dad could. It's not her fault, she's not had children, has she? We miss you and Mabel so much. We did ask Aunt Sylvie if you could come but she won't change her mind. Wilf says she will one day, he's going to make her.

The letters made Beau happy, but he ached, deep in the pit of his stomach; it made him want to run to her, to cheer her up in the way that only he could.

There aren't a lot of evacuees here. Me and Wilf really stand out in school. The other children think we talk and smell funny and they do these impressions of us that make Wilf's blood boil no matter how hard I tell him to calm down.

Mr Alford had stopped at this point. He looked like he had half a mind to hit the road and scoop his children up, but Beau wouldn't let him until he'd heard every word.

The one thing I like about Aunt Sylvie's house though is the lighthouse. It's right next to her cottage and, even though the lighthouse isn't that tall, on stormy nights, it sits up to attention, like you do, Beau, when you see a treat in my hand. I was worried when we got here that they wouldn't be allowed to light the lamp in a storm, you know, because it might help the German bombers find land easier, but they still do, just not as brightly as usual. What I love about it most is that when the light swings over the house, it lights up the road, down the way towards Swanage, and it's still strong enough that I imagine I can see all the way to Balham. In fact, I imagine that the next time the storm really rages, and the light hits the road, I'll see you, running towards me. I know it sounds silly, but it makes me feel happy and safe, like the war isn't really happening, like Hitler isn't really coming to hurt everyone.

I miss you all. Wilf says he hopes Mabel is missing him as much as he is her!

Your girl, Peggy.

Beau whimpered involuntarily, which earned him a scratch to his back, which, whilst pleasant, didn't ease the ache that he felt, right down to his very core. There was only one person who could cure that, and she felt a long, long way away.

12

London braced itself all winter long, but the skies remained empty, barring the birds that returned in the spring.

People became confused, dubious; some doubted that the aerial onslaught was ever coming and gave it a name: the Phoney War.

Without the gas attacks and bomb debris and chaos expected, some lost patience, and called their children home. Beau watched from the front windowsill, and by Easter, the faded chalk goalposts and hopscotch grids had reappeared, along with laughter and tears as matches were fought and knees skinned.

It raised Beau's hopes dramatically. Every time he saw a small person clutching a suitcase and a wide, relieved grin, he thought it might be Peggy, or Wilf, but it was always merely that: a thought. His girl remained nowhere to be seen.

He listened to every scrap of news he could: on the wireless of course, but most importantly, from Mr and Mrs Alford. They debated and discussed at length whether they should bring Peggy and Wilf home, their opinions swinging like the pendulum in the hallway's clock.

One minute it felt safe, the next it didn't.

'I hear things, don't I?' said a confused Mr Alford.

'From other wardens. News that it's just around the corner. That we haven't got a hope of defending ourselves, that the Luftwaffe is bigger and angrier than anything we even imagined.'

'But we've been hearing that for months,' Mrs Alford replied, tearfully, 'and I'm starting to forget what their voices sound like. I mean, I'll always be grateful to your Sylvie for what she's done . . . but she's not their mother. I am. And she won't really know when they need her most. She's not built for it, is she?'

That was impossible to disagree with (and Beau whimpered that she was right), but so was the news filtering down. The guidance remained the same. The city was on high alert, and it was no place for children, no matter how well-behaved they were, or how much their dogs missed them.

By the summer, the war was much more real. France had fallen, and then the Channel Islands. The Nazis were sweeping closer and Beau could feel the anxiety rising in the Alfords. The Battle of Britain was raging as the Nazi Luftwaffe tried to wipe out the Royal Air Force. Bomber was full of heroic tales of dogfights he'd witnessed between British Spitfires and Nazi Messerschmitts up in the skies.

The letters continued to arrive, with tales of Wilf spotting German planes in the lighthouse's beams. He'd thrown stones at them with all his might but only made contact with a window, which had not washed well with Aunt Sylvie.

Mrs Alford was in a terrible state after that letter. 'They're seeing planes down there? Well, then they'd be safer back here. We're not seeing any enemy planes.'

And it was true. Many a time the sirens went off and everyone trooped down to their air raid shelters, but there were no bombing raids over Balham. Mr Alford though was convinced that they were coming. That London would be hit and the children were safer away from the city.

There *were* positives to report in Peggy's letters, intermittently. One had told of another evacuee who'd arrived, from Wapping.

Alice is her name, it read, *Alice Quantrill. She's my age, and my height, and boy is she smart. She's read just about every book ever written. But she's not all girly, she's tough too. You should see her in the playground with a football at her feet. Them boys don't know how to stop her.*

This news had pleased Beau, warmed him, despite setting off an uncomfortable swirl of jealousy deep in his gut. He told himself that he wasn't to be so silly. That this was exactly what Peggy needed, and this Alice was all well and good, but no one could replace him in her true affections.

He felt doubly guilty when a letter arrived some weeks on, telling him that:

Alice has gone. Just like that. Overnight. Her mother came for her, told her she'd be safer at home. It's made me sad, I can't lie, all I want is to come back too: for Ma's pie, for Pa's jokes,

*but especially for you, Beau. Cos let's face it, we don't even
know how old you actually are, so every minute I don't get to
be with you feels like a waste. I'm sad about Alice, truly I am,
but not as sad as I am when I'm not with you. With all of
you. Please let me come home. Please.*

That particular letter left the house in the most sombre of
moods.

'I want to be with her,' sobbed Mrs Alford. 'She needs us.
They both do. It's been too long already.'

'Then we'll go down next month in the half term holiday.
We'll save up the fares and put ourselves up in a hotel nearby
and you can hug them everyday. How does that sound?'

Mrs Alford's eyes glistened and she reached for her
husband's hand. 'Wonderful!'

The Alfords' longing had never been so great, but as their
plans formed, everything escalated. For on the seventh of
September, war seemed to land right on top of them.

And it wasn't just the Blitz that started, but the remarkable
next chapter of Beau's rich life.

13

It was 4 p.m. when the sirens sounded, shocking Mrs Alford so badly that she peeled her forefinger instead of the potato in her hand. The potato dropped to the floor like a grenade and rolled under the sideboard. Satisfied that it wouldn't explode, and rightly worried that her house *might*, Mrs Alford wrapped a tea towel round her weeping knuckle and set about readying herself.

They were well-versed in what to do. Sirens had been going off all summer but with no room in the yard for their own Anderson shelter, and the local shelter so packed, they headed to Balham underground station, a brisk four-minute walk away.

But before that, they needed to round up the animals. Or at least try to. They had debated long and hard in the early days about what to do with Mabel.

'They won't allow animals underground, you know?' Mr Alford had warned his wife. 'People are angry enough that we didn't have them put down, without bringing them during a raid.'

'People can think what they want,' she had answered. 'We promised the children we'd try and keep them safe.'

That was fine with regards to Mabel. They had a wicker

basket they could hide her in (if she decided to keep quiet about it), but Beau was another matter. They had no basket big enough to house him, so it had been agreed that Beau would accompany Mr Alford on his warden duties – which he'd regularly been doing over the summer. It might not have been army work, but someone had to make sure lights were out, and people were safely underground.

Beau wasn't troubled by this. He didn't want to go in the underground station, he didn't trust the smell of it: there was a staleness to the air belching from its depths that reminded him of his time spent sleeping in alleyways.

Mabel wasn't keen on the idea of the basket either (this did *not* surprise Beau). In fact, she'd made it perfectly clear on the night of the first siren that she would neither go quietly, nor at all, bolting for the front door as soon as Mr Alford had teased it open.

'Mabel!' Mrs Alford had hollered. 'Get back here.' But it was fruitless, Mabel had chosen to take her chances on the streets, and nothing Mrs Alford could say, or offer as a treat, would tempt her back.

Tonight was no different. She dashed away as usual when the basket appeared. 'We'll have to leave her. It's probably for the best,' said Mr Alford, passing his wife her coat, which was instantly stained by her peeled knuckle. 'Do you need a bandage?'

'We haven't time,' she replied quickly. 'Or it'll be more than a finger that needs glueing back on.'

So with a final slam of the door, the Alfords and Beau raced to the station, along with the rest of the road. But although people had been doing this all summer, there was something more urgent in the air tonight. Beau could smell fear, and it seemed to be contagious. Beau could see how scared the adults were. How desperate to get to safety.

The few children around, though, didn't seem as perturbed. Babes in arms either slept on or were swaddled tightly, whilst the others seemed to look around with wide eyes, like it was the start of another enormous game.

People swarmed from everywhere, and by the time the station hoved into view, it was clear just how busy the platforms were going to be.

'Do you think there'll be room for me today?' She looked understandably anxious. Mr Alford knew he could try to use his position as warden if he wished, to escort his wife to the front of the snaking, unruly queue, but when he reluctantly suggested it, his wife put him straight.

'I'd be as uncomfortable with that as you, my love,' she replied, squeezing his hand. 'They'll make room, don't worry. Might just be a squeeze, that's all. Now, get on with you. There'll be folk need you more than me, I'm sure.'

So after a further firm word, and a loving embrace, Mr Alford straightened his tin helmet, turned and strode away to do his duty, with Beau following obediently behind. The crowds flooded onto the roads, which incensed the drivers of vans and carts who were understandably keen to finish their

61

journeys as quickly as possible. Seeing the danger, Mr Alford strode to where the congestion was heaviest, attracting the crowd's attention as best he could.

Had he shouted, it would've inevitably brought on a coughing fit, so instead, he pulled from his warden's box the most unlikely of tools: a wooden football rattle, which he'd used a few times over the summer.

Holding it above his head, he shook his wrist, and a noise exploded that was as incongruous as the air raid siren itself.

'Come on now, folks!' he gasped, breathing deeply to swallow any cough that might undermine him. 'Keep on the pavement. There's plenty of room if we just keep moving.'

But no matter how loudly he tried to shout, it was difficult to keep order. The siren wailed mercilessly around him, and when added to the general volume of panic and fear, he and his rattle felt insignificant.

Spotting Mr Alford's frustration, not to mention the sweat breaking across his cheeks, Beau leaped into action and took on warden duties himself. He sought out the ankles of the worst offenders, snapping and snarling at them until they danced their way onto the kerb. One after another, they jumped to the pavement, and whilst they may have been surprised by the unlikely sheepdog at their heels, everyone obeyed his orders.

Mr Alford was impressed by Beau's actions, joining the dog on the road, rattle spinning with vim and gusto, a voice belying his asthma.

'That's it, folks,' he yelled. 'Underground's only a hundred yards now, almost there. Form an orderly queue, please.'

The people scurried on, disappearing eventually through the bottleneck, like water down a plughole, until only a trickle remained.

'Well,' Mr Alford said. 'That was mighty impressive, Beau.'

Beau sat to attention, chest proudly puffed.

'We'll make a soldier out of you yet, I reckon. Wait till we tell Peggy.'

Beau didn't want to get carried away. He knew this was only the start of things. But there could be no doubt that he wanted his Peggy to be proud.

And a soldier, him? Wait until he told Bomber. The bird would fall clean off his perch.

14

That night was the start of Beau's basic military training. There were no army drills or passing out parades, only panic and thunder and destruction. Day after day, night after night, the streets of London were terrified by the banshee wail of the siren.

They're coming, they're coming! it cried, and it was not wrong. The bombs rained down night after night over London. The Nazis bulged with confidence after every raid, not always waiting for the cover of darkness to do their worst. If people dared to relax or exhale, if they dreamed of a night of unbroken sleep in their own beds without being woken to find the horizon not just changed but obliterated, then they were fools. The Blitz had begun.

The German bombers came again and again and again, until the date didn't seem to matter any more. All Londoners knew as the sun rose on more rubble and gas and fear, all they needed to know was that another day of bombing lay ahead. All they needed to be was ready.

Beau certainly was, despite a distinct lack of sleep. Mr Alford too, in spite of the bags under his eyes, and lungs irritated by constant dust and destruction. Night after night, Mr Alford assisted the weak, reassured the frightened, gave hope to the hopeless and searched for the dead. And then as the all-clear siren wailed, he would be waiting with Beau at the mouth of Balham station for his wife. She'd appear, eyes squinting against the milky sun, skin blanched spectre white by both the darkness below and the fear she'd felt.

She would always smile as soon as she locked eyes with him, and depending on the difficulty of the night, would either wipe the raid's dark smudges from his cheeks, or fall into his arms, sobbing. Beau could never quite tell if it were due to the horrors she'd heard overhead, or the relief that her beloved was still alive. Either way, it filled him with admiration and love for them both, reminding him why his Peggy had turned out to be so decent and loving.

Beau learned a lot from Mr Alford. He became his shadow while the siren sang, always at his heel, quick to offer a reassuring bark when the man's cough overwhelmed him, yet always watching too, witnessing his kindness, and especially his dedication. More and more often they were called to houses that had crumbled beneath the Nazis' anger, and with every house they visited, Mr Alford seemed to shrink an inch. Beau saw it in his sagging shoulders and deeply creasing brow. It was hard to reconcile that the rubble had once been a home, a place of safety and protection. It horrified both man and dog to think that people may still be lying trapped beneath it.

'There can't be anyone left under there,' other wardens would say.

But Mr Alford had no time for such talk. 'Would you want

folk to give up on you that easily? Isn't there a chance, no matter how small, that there could be life in there? Because if there is, then we shouldn't give up, not yet.'

Sometimes, this would be enough to see the other men dig and probe with him, tossing aside roof tiles and children's toys in the hope of revealing a twitching leg or waving hand. Other times, he would be left on his own to search, except he was never truly alone, because he had Beau beside him, and what the dog lacked in hands, he made up for with the keenest of noses.

It was some three weeks into what felt like the endless Blitz, when Beau proved once and for all that Peggy was right to save his life. He and Mr Alford had been called to a terrace off Bedford Hill, which had been hit heavily overnight. A cluster of houses, reduced to nought. Cigarettes smouldered in the rescuers' mouths, despite the smell of gas thick in the air.

'Put those out!' scolded Mr Alford, Beau barking if they refused to do as they were told. 'Now, how many residents aren't accounted for?'

'The Hellons at number fourteen,' a woman replied, face white with either shock or dust. 'Didn't make it to the underground, apparently. They're a family of four but the little'uns had a fever and were too ill to go. They decided to stay at home and take their chances. God bless 'em.'

'Number fourteen?' said Mr Alford, placing a comforting arm on the distressed neighbour.

But so crumpled were the houses, Mr Alford had no idea

where number fourteen might begin or end. Only a pointed finger told him where he should be looking, and he started straight away, using the blunt end of his ceiling pike to prod and poke at gaps, to expose pockets of air or trapped limbs. Others joined in, pulling at bricks and splintered window frames. None of it had any real strategy to it, apart from the work that Beau was undertaking.

Nose to the ground, he sniffed every inch, but not indiscriminately. Instead, he followed closely behind Mr Alford, taking the time to mirror his path, inhaling and understanding the smells aroused by his prodding, even if it was only dust that clogged his nostrils until he sneezed. But then, some thirty minutes in, as others were declaring it 'fruitless', or more crudely, 'a waste of bleedin' time', Beau hit upon something. It seemed like nothing at first, nothing distinctive anyway, then, mixed in with the dust, there was another smell. Something sweeter, something that he thought, no, *knew*, was alive. Pushing his nose deeper into the rubble despite its sharp edges, the scent grew stronger and more distinct. There was something down there, he knew it. It was just like the hiding games with Peggy, where he could sense a child as they crouched behind the door of the lav.

He pulled aside a rock with his paws, then a second and a third which he dislodged with his jaws and muzzle. The smell grew stronger still, as did the pounding of his heart. He scrabbled some more, until he moved nothing but dust, his claws coming up against a large slab of concrete. He tried again and again to no avail, but he could not stop, the scent was too strong, filling him with determination and hope. There was someone down there, he knew it, just *knew* it. So he did what he had to, and tried to tell Mr Alford, his bark cutting through the dust like a beam of light.

'What is it, Beau?' he wheezed in return, bent double over his pike. 'Come on, get away from there. I've already searched it.' He pulled out his handkerchief, wiping impotently at the dust on his brow.

Beau barked again. He knew Mr Alford had searched, but he hadn't found them, had he? And now he *had* and it was as clear as day. There was someone down here. Someone worth saving. But no matter how many times he barked, nobody took any notice. Another warden had arrived, a tall man with a pencil of a moustache, and he was now telling Mr Alford to move on, that there were other houses needing searching for possible life, three streets down. Dutifully, Mr Alford went to follow him and called Beau to heel, which he did obediently, *too* obediently, scampering up to him and nipping the bottom of his trouser leg.

'Beau!' he shouted. 'Stop that! We've no time to play, not now.'

Beau clung on and backed away, pulling Mr Alford with him.

'Beau, that's ENOUGH!' But it wasn't. Nowhere near. And the more he resisted, the harder Beau pulled, not stopping until the pair of them were standing back over the spot where he had chanced upon the smell. Finally, letting go of the trouser leg, Beau dug again, scrabbling with a ferocity that no one could ignore. Apart from the pencil-tached man.

'Alford. You coming, or not?'

This was a moment. A moment when Mr Alford could've ignored the dog, dismissing his actions as folly. But for some reason, he didn't. Instead, he watched Beau's urgency and believed in him, yelling back, 'Not yet. We've found something. Beau's found something.'

And he dropped to his knees, pulling at the stone that had thwarted his daughter's pet. As it moved, the smell grew stronger, to Beau at least, hitting him with a clarity that made him dig on. Away came more dust and rocks, and with Mr Alford beside him, in tandem they tore at the earth, until finally, they saw it. A hand, dusty and bloodied, but a hand nonetheless.

Mr Alford's mouth fell open in surprise. 'There's a hand,' he cried to anyone who would listen. 'Come here! Come quick, there's someone down here!' He watched as Beau licked at the fingers, not believing his eyes when he saw them twitch, not once, but twice. 'Sweet Jesus, they're ALIVE!'

And that was it. They were the only words those milling around needed to hear, and they dashed beside them, forming a chain, removing every chunk of brick until the hand became an arm, and the arm an upper body.

'Careful now!' insisted Mr Alford, as the neck and head were finally unveiled. 'It's a girl, and she's bleeding.' She was too, a large gash by her right eye the only source of colour on her ashen face. Beau was tempted to lick her clean, but by then, an ambulance crew had arrived and were surrounding the girl, checking her pulse and pushing a swab to her temple.

'Steady now,' they cried. 'There's a pulse, but it's weak, any more shocks might end her.'

But as the medics lifted the girl onto the stretcher and stumbled towards the ambulance, Beau smelled something else, a trace of something or, more importantly, someone. Taking six paces to his left, he sniffed the earth long and deep, then started to dig again with both of his front paws. He didn't stop until he had everyone's attention, and, more importantly, their help.

15

'So you're a soldier now?' said Bomber, without a shred of bitterness or jealousy in his voice. 'A hero, in fact!' If anything, he sounded proud, like he was seeing Beau with fresh eyes.

'I'd hardly say that,' Beau replied bashfully, pretending to wash his front paws. 'I was just in the right place at the right time.'

'That's not what I heard. My brother, Titch, he was taking a rest on a telegraph pole by Bedford Hill, said he saw it all unfold. You with your bum in the air, digging and digging until you found what you were after.'

'I'm not sure it was really like that.'

'And what's all this about biting your master till he listened to you? Beyond brave, that is.'

'Foolish, some would say,' said Mabel, who had slyly positioned herself on the wall, eavesdropping as always.

Her arrival made Beau stand up for himself and tell his version of the story.

'Well, Mr Alford is a good man, but he wasn't to know my nose is . . . well . . . sensitive. I knew I'd found something. I just had to make him realise. And once I found *one* person, well, I guessed there would be another . . .'

'And another and another!' laughed Bomber. 'Four of them, you found, didn't you?'

'Don't ask him that,' yawned Mabel. 'He can't count to two, never mind higher.'

'That's right, Bomber,' said Beau, aiming a firm stare in Mabel's direction. 'Parents and two children. The boy didn't look too clever, but he's still fighting apparently.'

'A doctor now too, are you, as well as a hero?' spat Mabel. She laced the last word with as much sarcasm as she could possibly fit on her rough tongue.

'Hardly. I just heard the Alfords talking about it. At supper. You'd have heard the same thing if you ever bothered to come home.'

'If I come home, they'll stuff me in that prison of a basket in a flash. And I'm not having that. There's more fun and better food to be found in the great outdoors, you know.'

Although it sounded ridiculous, it was true. With animals, cats in particular, having been put to sleep in their thousands, London's mouse and rat populations were thriving. Mabel's burgeoning belly proved it, and judging from her heavy eyelids, she'd just feasted in spectacular fashion.

'What about you, Bomber?' Beau asked. 'Any news on your conscription?'

'Nothing concrete,' he replied, seeing it as his cue to strut the length of the coop's roof, fluffing his wings. 'But it's coming, I can tell. You don't come from a long line of soldiers like I do and not see action. Plus,' he motioned to the house, 'him indoors is flying us more than ever, longer and longer distances, and when I see how the others are struggling to keep up? Well, there's no doubt that when those colonels and generals come knocking, it will be for me. I'll be a general myself in no time.'

'I don't doubt it for a second,' said Beau, and he really meant it, despite the sniggering coming from Mabel.

'Listen to the pair of you. You're animals. Leave the fighting to the humans, we're smart enough to know there's no point in wars.'

Beau laughed, remembering the number of times she'd bared her claws or teeth in his direction. But before he could pull the hypocrite up, the siren announced itself, no less shocking than the first time they'd heard it.

Beau wasn't scared though. Not any more. He was prepared. He was already at the door, scratching at it to be by Mr Alford's side. It opened suddenly to reveal Mrs Alford clutching the wicker basket, which as always was Mabel's cue to leap out of sight. She'd catch no mice while stuck in there, and she was already feeling peckish again.

And Bomber? Bomber looked to the skies through narrowed eyes, heart throbbing. His time was coming. He was sure of it.

16

No two bombing raids were the same: different times, different streets, but the end result was the same. Chaos, flames, gas, fear.

The other thing that came with them, inevitably, was death. It was everywhere Mr Alford and Beau looked. Bodies laid out under sheets, wreaths left stranded on front steps, although no discernible house was left behind them.

It wasn't just lives that were lost, it was histories too. No matter what people grabbed when the sirens howled, there wasn't time or space in their hands to carry everything of value, whether financial or emotional, and as a result, in a split second, families' memories and legacies were lost for ever. People sifted through rubble and at times got lucky: a photograph album here, a silver candlestick there, but they were always tainted, and not just by the dust that covered them. They were also a reminder of everything else that was lost.

It was overwhelming to witness, and Beau could tell that Mr Alford tried not to dwell too long on it. He had a job to do and, as hard as it was, he had to swallow down every bit of emotion he felt. In doing so, he kept his eyes clear and his hopes high. But afterwards, Beau could feel the sadness in this good man in the way he stroked Beau or sighed as they walked home together.

After a bombing, as soon as the rubble had stopped burning, and the firemen had declared it safe to enter, Mr Alford and Beau set about their work: Mr Alford probing gently with his pike, Beau putting his nose to the ground and searching for any sign of life, no matter how fragile its condition.

He found it too. Night after night, explosion after explosion, ruin after ruin. It didn't always happen quickly, but it happened, and with miraculous regularity.

A wonderful yield would be a person of any age, their chests moving faintly like a fledgling found in an upturned nest. But there were also nights when Beau happened upon entire families, clutching each other beneath a fractured dining table or door, clinging to life as well as each other.

What became apparent was that it wasn't just Beau's nose that was to be celebrated, it was his stubbornness. There were times, especially in the early weeks, when the wardens called it a night: when they refused point blank to believe that anyone, or anything could be left intact beneath the devastation. But as they wiped their brows and collected their tools, Beau showed no such resignation. Instead, he prowled, nose to the dirt, ignoring every attempt to call him to heel. A less patient master might have become irritable, angry even, but not his. Mr Alford had seen the good in this dog already, not just amongst the wreckage, but with his daughter, and he quickly and wisely made the decision to trust him. If Beau said there was reason to continue, then he would not argue, he would simply assist.

The results were extraordinary, his tenacity rewarded. Site after site, time after time, they happened upon lives buried deep in the chaos. And even though precious few were awake to thank him, Beau pressed on. He didn't want congratulating. He didn't want anything but to trust what his senses were telling him, and he wouldn't stop until they told him there was nothing left to find.

'That's an extraordinary hound you've got there. What breed is he?' It was a question Mr Alford was asked a lot. And whilst at first he had no answer, after a time he knew exactly what to say. 'Pedigree lifesaver, he is. Purebreed.'

People would often nod, like they'd heard of the breed themselves, which always made Beau chuckle to himself. As did the spoils of his work, which often appeared the following day with a knock at their door.

'Dog biscuits for the war hero,' they'd say as they bent to thank Beau. Or, 'Bit of scrag end – it's not all fat.'

Beau didn't quite know what to make of the adulation. He didn't ask for it, nor bathe in it, though he did take delight in seeing the effect it had on Mabel – her disgusted and envious face was always a joy, as was the fact that she wasn't allowed to partake in what had been brought.

'Hey now, that's Beau's biscuit,' Mr Alford would chide. 'The second you start finding life instead of gallivanting, then you can join in with the party.'

That always went down well – usually with a hiss or a bat of her claws the next time Beau happened to pass too close to her.

It didn't take long for Beau's fame to spread beyond the realms of Balham. As the bombing intensified, and the East End saw a fury like nothing witnessed outside the gates of Hell, Mr Alford and Beau were called over to Wapping to help with the aftermath and the hunt for survivors. After one ferocious night, where street upon street had been levelled, the pair found themselves picking their way through various sites. The devastation broke something in Beau. The night sky looked huge with no buildings to interrupt it, and apart from the pungent whiff of gas and burned timber, there was precious little else, certainly very few aromas of life.

How could humans do that to one another? he thought to himself, but it didn't stop him trying to save them. That first night, he discovered a family trapped deep within the remains of their house. While the breath had been snuffed from the parents, they had managed to protect their daughter, throwing themselves on top of her, bearing the brunt of the falling beams and leaving a trace of life within her that Beau was delirious to sniff out. He watched as the wardens carefully dug her free, hearing a cry from behind him as a neighbour gasped in relief.

'That's Syd!' she cried. 'Oh praise God, she's alive.'

Whilst Beau was happy, and relieved that the girl was alive, he felt sadness too at what lay ahead for her.

It also pricked his thoughts for Peggy. Was she safe? And if she was, was she thriving? Or even happy? He didn't like to think of her as lonely, and homesick, and he couldn't imagine that Wilf would offer much in the way of comfort.

It took a bomb exploding in the distance, over towards Shadwell Basin, to pull Beau out of the daydream.

'Come, Beau, come,' Mr Alford said, tapping his thigh gently.

Beau didn't need telling twice. He was already following the angry orange flames that danced mercilessly across the sky.

17

October brought swollen skies and fierce winds that chilled Beau to his core.

He was lucky then that his new-found celebrity didn't just mean edible gifts (though he was always grateful for them). It also meant a very special present from one grateful young survivor. It was a tunic of sorts, stitched from a long piece of sacking. Whilst it was hardly silk, it *was* thick and warm, and the scratchiness of the fabric couldn't force its way beyond his wiry hair. If anything, it seemed to insulate him, cutting out the wind chill almost entirely. What he liked most about it (apart from the strokes from the girl as she'd dressed him up), were the additions that she'd sewn onto it. On its back (presumably to face the bombers as they taunted from above), was a large red cross, which made Beau unbelievably proud. It showed his credentials as a canine first aider, but it also made him feel indestructible.

'Look at him!' Mr Alford said proudly. 'A four-legged St George. Slay a dragon, he could, dressed in that!'

The flourish that Beau loved even more wasn't visible to the airborne Germans, though. It was stitched on his chest, next to his heart. It was a medal, made from a red ribbon and a golden paper circle (stolen from a pre-war Christmas chocolate). It rustled whenever he moved, a constant reminder that he was a good boy, the best of boys, and that he was doing everything his Peggy had asked of him. He was keeping people safe wherever and whenever he could, and he wished more than anything that she could see the medal as it clung to him.

It was lucky then that his exploits had grabbed the attention of the local newspaper, who wanted to share his bravery with their readers. The first thing the Alfords knew of it was a rap at the door, where a young man stood, looking like he should've been finishing his homework rather than wielding a camera.

'Is this where the dog lives?' he asked, meekly.

Beau looked at him from between Mr Alford's legs.

'Depends which one you mean?' Mr Alford replied.

'The bomb dog. The one that, you know . . . finds all those bodies.' He looked a little queasy, the poor lamb, so Beau put him out of his misery with a quick, friendly bark, and a lick of his hand, which saw the boy take a fearful step backwards.

Thirty painful minutes later, the lad had stumbled through all his questions and reached for his camera, positioning Mr Alford and Beau at the front door, the pair of them resplendent in their warden overalls and knight's tunic. Beau made sure his medal was on full display.

'Do you think I could get a print of the photo?' Mr Alford asked.

'I'd have thought so,' replied the boy with little certainty.

Although his answer was far from definitive, it was enough to make Mr Alford traipse to the newspaper offices each day, until finally, he held the photo in his hand, proud as punch.

Propping it up against the salt cellar on the kitchen table, he started to pen a letter to Peggy, telling her all about her brave dog.

Dearest Peggy, he wrote, reading out loud.

Beau's fame continues to grow, and no mistake. This photograph is the result of an interview with the South London Press, and whilst they are yet to publish the article (the reporter seemed little older than you!), I will make sure to send it on when they do.

Peggy, you would be so proud of your Beau. He is not only the finest of companions, but the bravest of dogs. No, of any living thing you could wish to meet.

Things here are . . .

He sucked on his pen as he searched for the right word. It *had* to be the right one, so as not to scare Peggy.

Beau only wished he could help.

. . . challenging. Challenging enough that it gives your mum and me the feeling that sending you two away, as hard as it is, was the right thing to do.

But one of the things that gives us most strength and happiness, besides you and Wilf being safe, is seeing how the animals cope with everything. Mabel (you won't be surprised to hear) deals with it as only Mabel can. She hunts. I've never seen a cat catch as many mice or rats as her, and she is always so generous with the half-eaten treats she leaves for us, on the back step or hearth! I'm surprised your mum hasn't broken all of our kitchen chairs by jumping on them. I feel like I could draw every internal organ a rodent owns, now I've seen so many of them.

As for your Beau, well, he is extraordinary. Never flinches at the sound of the siren or a bomb. If anything, he grows bigger. Braver. Puts his nose to the rubble and doesn't stop until he knows no life is left trapped. It's extraordinary, Peg. His patience, stubbornness, even. Nothing could drag him away if he believes a heart is still beating beneath the rubble. And so now, when he digs, I dig with him. He gives the orders to stop, not me. And as a result, when I'm with him, I feel safe too.

I can't say that rescuing folks makes him happy. There's only one thing that could make him so, and that's you. But it makes his life bearable, gives it meaning, until you see each other once more. And you know what? He's right, isn't he? We have to take comfort where we can right now, and I know, I KNOW, that no matter what happens from this point on, while we have this dog, then you'll be all right. And that makes me happy too.

Tell me your news. I hope the lighthouse at Anvil Point is shining on you all, keeping you safe.

With love, write soon. Oh, and Beau sends his love (of course),

Mum and Dad, Beau and Mabel.
Xx

Mr Alford read the letter to Beau and then, after tipping a small pool of ink onto a saucer, he carefully took hold of the dog's paw.

'Trust me, Beau. It's all fine,' he whispered. The dog was a willing accomplice. After dipping his paw in the ink, he turned the letter over and pressed it firmly to Beau's black pads. What it left behind was perfection: a message from Beau.

Beau watched Mr Alford slide it into the envelope, having carefully blown the ink dry.

Peggy would be thrilled. He felt closer to her now than he had in over a year.

If only that feeling would last.

18

Waiting for replies was painful, as mail deliveries could be sporadic. Little wonder given how many men had been 'posted' overseas.

Beau would wait every morning on the front step, not unlike many others who lived on Boundaries Road. Life had to go on while loved ones fought, but it wasn't easy, not knowing if they were safe, under fire, already hurt.

When the postie *did* arrive, Beau would bound down the path to the gate, front paws on the wood. There were days, too many of them for Beau's liking, where he was met by a shake of the head and a 'Nothing today', but the days when an envelope was slid into his jaws? They were heavenly.

Beau's heart would flip and his head spin as he awaited the news that lay inside. He would take the letter straight to the Alfords, depositing it on a lap before sitting obediently, so as not to give them a reason to delay.

The letters always started the same way: *Dearest Beau,* at which point Beau always held his breath as he waited for the tone of her words.

Winter is definitely biting here.
Even when the sun is out, it doesn't seem to reach as high

in the sky. And as a result, it's quieter. The beaches, the
seafront. Everywhere, really. You see, the summer made it
easier. There were more children, a few day-trippers, and
unlike the children at school, who still seem to think I'm from
another planet, they were always happy to play with us, even
Wilf. You'd have loved the beach, Beau. There was plenty of
Hide and Seek going on, though not much skipping, but
imagine the holes you could've dug? All the way to Australia,
knowing you! The days seemed to go on for ever, and they were
so busy, it gave us something else to think about other than
missing you all. It also gave us time away from Aunt Sylvie
too. I think we tire her out. Wilf especially. She says we don't,
but once she's served tea, she disappears into the sitting room
while we wash up. It doesn't matter if the dishes take us ten
minutes or thirty, by the time we tiptoe in to find her, she's
always asleep. Wilf likes finding different things to tickle
under her nose, to see which makes her wake up most suddenly
and noisily. Not that she'll ever admit she was dozing – 'I was
just resting my eyes', she says, or 'I was having ten minutes for
half an hour'. Makes me laugh, it does, to see Wilf trying to
work out the maths behind that one.

But enough of that. Thank you for the last letter, and for
the pawprint!! I've put it by my bed, so it's the first and last
thing I see every day.

It doesn't surprise me, Beau, that you are being so brave.
You must promise me though, that you are being careful, you
and Dad both. Of course I want you to help people, but if

something was to happen to either of you? Well, I don't know what I would do. So promise me, every time you go digging, you'll do it with one eye looking over your shoulder. All of us, we just need to stay safe, so we can be together again soon.

Write to me again, I'm waiting impatiently for the next of your stories.

With love from your girl,
Peggy.
Xx

19

Beau didn't like it.

The siren wasn't wailing any louder than normal, nor did the air smell any different. He sensed panic, and sweat, and fear, but that was normal, to be expected.

He didn't like the queues outside the underground station. People, scared to death by a month of endless shelling, had started taking shelter in the tunnels even when the siren was silent.

It drove Mr Alford to distraction. 'Selfishness, it is. Pure selfishness. There's room for everyone who needs to shelter. I mean, there's folks down there with mattresses and tea services.'

'It's all right, love,' his wife replied. 'As you say, there's space. We just have to be patient.'

But Mr Alford was unusually short of it tonight. Beau could feel the tension in him, the exhaustion. He looked too tired to even clear his lungs, and when his wife reached the front of the queue, their embrace was longer than usual, as if they were preparing each other for the difficulty of the night ahead.

Finally, after their hug ended, Mr Alford and Beau watched her be swallowed by the station and they turned to face Balham High Road, where a Jurassic-length snake of people trailed as far as the eye could see. It would be dark soon, so they both knew they had one job: to clear the streets before that happened and the enemy bombardment began.

They cajoled and rallied, they encouraged and chastised, not stopping until the python had slithered underground and they could embark on their rounds, checking folk were safe in their own backyard shelters, that all lights had been extinguished and the blackout was complete.

As early evenings went, it was uneventful, and Beau felt the foreboding ease a little. People were compliant, lights were switched off, and aside from the occasional bus ferrying the last of the stragglers to their homes, the roads were quiet. The skies, too.

But only minutes after 8 p.m., Hitler unleashed Hell in the shape of a bomb that tore the sky apart, ripping it in two like a piece of cloth.

Beau heard it, or heard something at least: a whistle, which became a whine and then a banshee's wail. It tore at his ears as he stood in the middle of Balham High Road, eyes following the blur as it fell to earth.

The world seemed to stop in the final seconds as the truth finally hit him, only to then accelerate into a tornado of noise which tossed him off his feet and into a shop front some thirty feet away.

He may have blacked out. He couldn't be sure. It didn't seem to matter. He felt his legs tremble and he winced as he pushed them straight, then thrust his nose into the thick cloying dust that had enveloped him.

It would've been easier to ball himself up in the shop doorway: to lick his wounds and allow the humans to try and tidy up the mess of their own creation, but he couldn't do that. He didn't have it in him, and Peggy wouldn't want it that way. Because somewhere out there, in the dust cloud, was her father. All that mattered in that moment was finding him.

So Beau searched, despite the gloom, despite the sound of masonry crumbling around him, coating him in dust and grime. He heard cries and screams, the crackle of burning buildings, the long, loud wail of a van's horn, but he let nothing disturb him. He had to find Mr Alford, there was no other mission to undertake.

He stumbled around, splintered glass pressing deep into his pads, testing their resilience. But just as he feared his senses had been scrambled by the explosion, he found something. Not much, not even a smell, but a trace: of Brylcreem, the same oil that Mr Alford used to slick back his hair. It wasn't rare, many men slaked their head in the same stuff, but that didn't put Beau off, it was all he had and he had to hope it was enough.

He shoved his nose down to the ground. The scent faded. He backtracked. It increased. It was trial and error, like a sick game of Blind Man's Buff, but Beau didn't give up when he hit a dead end. He pushed on, accelerating when he hit a new sweet spot.

There it was again. Stronger. Stronger still. He could practically taste it. It had to be him, had to be. His nose went down, his tail up like an antenna. He was in the road now, sniffing his way past a car blown onto its side, the roof sheared off like it had been clumsily opened by a child with a tin opener.

And there he was: Mr Alford, sitting up against the chassis, overalls grey where they had once been blue, a large crescent dent in his helmet which somehow, thankfully, remained fastened to his head.

Beau bounded to him, sniffing every inch for damage, sensing no blood or broken bones, though he only knew for sure when Mr Alford launched into a chesty cacophony of sound, spraying the air with yet more dust. He was alive, that was all that mattered and Beau proved it by licking frantically at his face, drawing more splutters and hacks.

'It's all right, Beau. I'm all right,' he said. 'Are you?' Beau felt hands all over him, blindly searching for cuts.

It was fine, he barked. He was fine.

Slowly, Mr Alford climbed to his feet, arms outstretched as he groped into the dust cloud.

'Can you see it, boy?' he asked. 'Did you see where it landed?'

Beau hadn't, but he could smell it. Dreadful, it was. Deathly. He smelled gas, fizzing into the air, and unless he was mistaken, water too, plenty of it. Taking care not to rush on ahead so Mr Alford could see him, he crept forward, zigzagging past hazards: a crumpled, displaced manhole cover, a lamppost now bent like a boomerang. He only stopped when he saw for the first time the damage that had been done. He had to stop, firstly because it took his breath away, and secondly because to plough on would've meant falling headfirst into the biggest crater Beau had ever seen.

For yards and yards it stretched, the entire width of Balham High Road, and just as long: a jagged hole that would've looked more in keeping on the surface of the moon. Pipes jutted and tangled, steel girders were held up by mere planks of wood that were splintering by the second. It hissed and spat, a mixture of the gas and water that poured out, almost loud enough to drown the strong words that fell from Mr Alford's mouth.

'Christ alive!' he yelled (amongst other things). 'God help us.'

Looking up, Beau realised that there, tipped into the middle of the hole, sat the most grotesque and incongruous sight: a crumpled Routemaster bus. And Lord knows how many people remained inside.

20

The bus didn't belong in the hole, it made no sense to either of them, but there wasn't a thing they could do about it except stare. It was almost submerged, the nose buried as deeply as Beau's around a foxhole. If it burrowed much further it would soon make contact with the underground tunnels below, and who knew how much carnage *that* might cause.

Mr Alford shouted behind him into the foggy darkness, but a mixture of dust and fear stopped his words coming and replaced them with a violent cough. Not that it mattered, help had already arrived, two panting men in similarly filthy overalls and helmets.

'Did you watch it go in?' one yelled. 'Never seen anything like it. The bus was prancing like a pony as it tried to avoid it. Terrifying.'

'People . . .' Mr Alford panted. 'The driver, passengers . . . onboard still.'

'It's not just the bus though, mate,' the other warden replied. 'It's underground we're worried about. The bomb's severed the main water pipe, gas too. We can't get down there, not yet, but it must be filling up, has to be!'

Beau saw Mr Alford's expression change – a ghastly mixture of anxiety, shock and blind panic. He could see his entire being yanked in one direction, to his wife below ground. Was she trapped, submerged, breathing in whatever foul air was being pumped around her?

Mr Alford turned away from the crater and took a step forward, but as he did so, there was a rumbling behind him, followed by a tremor that shook everything on four legs, never mind two. Without warning, the tarmac beneath them began to tremble, crumbling into the hole towards the bus, pulling at Mr Alford's heels as he tried to throw his momentum forward.

He was a thin man, a wisp, the years of asthma leaving him lacking the power to drive away from the hole, and within seconds it wasn't just his heels tipping backwards, but his toes, his calves, his waist, until all Beau could do, almost in sickly slow motion, was watch his master topple backwards, eyes wide and disbelieving.

Beau barked and howled, but it was fruitless. Mr Alford had disappeared from view entirely, tumbling into the depths of the crater below, sliding beneath the wheels of the bus.

Horror consumed Beau, the sound of Mr Alford's body hitting the rubble looping in his ears. He had to do something, to retrieve and lick the life back into him, but as he went to jump, he felt something stop him, two fingers tucked resolutely inside his collar.

He barked his disapproval. The warden held on tighter.

'Steady on, boy! It's not safe down there.'

Beau tried to tell him it didn't matter, but the man ignored him, holding on for grim life no matter how many times Beau barked or snarled.

''Ere, Jack,' the warden yelled to his comrade. 'You got that length of rope still? Bring it 'ere will you? This boy's got the devil in him. Desperate to get down there, he is!'

The man did as he was told, slipping the rope through Beau's collar, making a crude lead, though to the dog it felt like a noose.

'Come on, now. You can't follow him, you've got to let us do that.' The man cajoled and tugged with every sinew, but Beau dug in. He couldn't leave Mr Alford. Peggy would never forgive him. His claws scraped the tarmac, but once the second man joined in, his face red with exertion, Beau was powerless, and his paws skidded backwards until the men secured him to a lamppost on the kerbside.

Beau was furious. He howled and wailed, he bucked and writhed. How dare they? He could find Mr Alford quicker than them. He could still smell him, though the trace of him was fading by the second. If they'd just let him go, then it would be all right. He wouldn't let it be any other way. He watched as the first warden clambered into the hole, and knew instinctively he was going to the wrong part of the crater. Beau told him so, repeatedly, but every time the bark left him, Mr Alford's scent grew weaker. He was fading, Beau knew that, so he tugged and pulled at the lead, which never gave an inch. He wouldn't stop though, not until he was free. He'd pull the lamppost over if he had to. That or chew his way through the rope. Fortunately, after ten minutes of tenacious tugging, the knot the men had tied grew tired and gave up, allowing Beau to dash back to the crater, rope dragging behind him.

As his feet neared the hole though, the scent changed. He could still pick up the Brylcreem, but nothing else, or nothing that felt welcoming, or alive.

His pace quickened, a whimper escaping involuntarily. He was ready to jump. To plunge headfirst into the hole, where he would dig and dig and dig until Mr Alford was coughing safely in his care. But as he prepared to fly, he found there was no need, as a warden, leaning deep over the crater, started to straighten up, arms struggling with the deadest of weights.

No, thought Beau. No, no, no.

It didn't matter how many times he wished it otherwise, the sight in front of him could not and would not change: for in the warden's shaking arms lay the lifeless body of Mr Alford. Beau did all he could, as any good, loyal dog would, but though he whimpered and pawed at the man's chest, not a single breath was taken.

Mr Alford had passed, and Beau howled. At the injustice and his regret, but most of all, he howled for his Peggy.

21

Beau would not leave him. How could he?

Instead, he lay at his side, chin resting on Mr Alford's cold arm. He licked him every now and then too, not in some naïve attempt to flush life back into his body, but to keep the man's scent close for as long as he could. Although Beau's body was here, in London, his thoughts didn't stray once from Peggy. The pain she would feel when she found out. Well, he would feel it too, was feeling it already, and he vowed to be alongside Mrs Alford when she told the children.

Perhaps it might mean they would *all* stay by the coast, until the bombs stopped at least. That way he could help Peggy, protect her, just like she had him. It was scant solace at that moment, especially when two burly wardens approached with a stretcher, stumbling over the debris as they came. Beau had never seen them before in his life.

'Come on pooch, shift,' one said, whilst the other's bedside manner was little better, trying to shoo Beau away with the back of his hand. Beau snarled in reply.

'Listen,' the man grunted, 'if you want a kick then you're going the right way about it.' And he flicked a jagged piece of rubble straight at Beau with his boot, forcing him to retreat.

With little care, they bundled Mr Alford onto the stretcher, wobbling their way back towards the ambulance, looking several times as though they would drop him in their haste.

Beau darted around them, circling, telling them to show more respect, but this only seemed to rile them more, and when he tried to jump in the back of the ambulance too, their patience broke, one warden grabbing Beau by his scruff and tossing him onto the street like he was an empty bottle. Beau rolled, winded, but he did not shatter. They couldn't just take Mr Alford like that, not without him too, or at least without him saying a proper farewell. But as Beau bounded up to the back doors of the ambulance, he saw them swing shut, mere inches from taking the end of his muzzle with them.

The vehicle tore off, kicking yet more dust into the air. It settled, speck by speck on Beau's face like a mourner's veil.

But the arrival of a second ambulance quickly brought him to the realisation that there wasn't time for grieving. It pulled up in front of the entrance to the underground station with a screech.

Only then did Beau remember what the first wardens had said to Mr Alford, about the chaos that was going on below, the water and gas that were filling up the tunnels where people cowered, petrified. The tunnels where Mrs Alford was sheltering.

He was on his feet in a second, all thoughts of loss tossed back into the rubble. If he couldn't save Mr Alford, then he must, *must* find a way to his wife instead, and the only way to do that was to fill his nose with the scent of her.

There were so many smells that accompanied her. The beef dripping that she wiped from her hands to her pinny every Sunday, the soapy water she sluiced across the front step, the rose talcum powder she used after a bath. It gave him confidence, there was no way his nose would fail him when there were these and other strong aromas that clung to her wherever she went.

As his nose hit the entrance to the underground station, his senses were on high alert. There were so many scents that it felt impossible to separate them out, to pinpoint exactly where she might be hidden, but at least the air wasn't just saturated by the smell of death.

It wasn't easy to make progress down there. The scene was pure chaos. From the depths there surged a constant wave of people, some coughing, others weeping, all coated in dirt and mud and sewage.

Beau tried to scamper between their legs, but they came so thick and fast that he was inevitably knocked to the floor, again and again and again. He felt their boots against his fur, kicking his chest, his head, his rump, but every blow merely increased his determination. He knew she had not passed him yet, his nose would have told him so, and so on he went, navigating the stairs to the tunnel despite the tide still crashing against him.

He wasn't sure what to expect when he reached the bottom: this was his first adventure underground, but what he saw to his left was not what he had anticipated.

This was not a tunnel but a dead end, rubble and soil piled

high as on a freshly filled grave. He sniffed at it but got nothing but dirt. He raced down the right-hand tunnel instead, from where the stream of people was finally thinning. It was dark and murky, but more importantly, he couldn't smell a trace of hope in the air. Beau didn't let this stop him searching: thrusting his nose down every inch of the platform, sniffing at abandoned bags and coats, only stopping when he was finally convinced that his hunt was futile. She had to be on the other platform, *had to be*, and he set about burrowing his way through, ignoring the pain as his paws ripped at the rocks' sharp edges.

He made progress, bit by bit, but for every inch of dirt he dislodged, more fell from above it, filling in the gaps, taking him infuriatingly back to where he had started. It even fell on him, threatening to wedge him tightly and bury him alive.

He couldn't give up, wouldn't. She had to be in there, and if that was the case, so did he. But the rocks and bricks were unforgiving and cruel, and he felt his claws splinter against them, leaving his pads sore and chafed. He stopped long enough to lick an especially painful spot, but as he did so, he felt his world tilt and he was pulled back.

Was this it? Another bomb? But no, he quickly realised this was no explosion, just another ruddy-cheeked man in a warden's helmet, pulling the stub of his lead so roughly that he almost decapitated him.

Beau growled his displeasure but the man didn't care a jot.

'Christ on a bike! What you doing digging like that? You want the whole tunnel to come down?' He pulled Beau roughly again, bumping him up the stairs with such force that the dog expected each step to be imprinted on his haunches. He fought back, or tried to, but every struggle seemed to pull his collar tighter, making it harder and harder to breathe. All he wanted to do was get to Mrs Alford, but nobody seemed to understand that. He saw colours change before his eyes, wondered if this was the end, before realising he was back at the surface, and the lights were merely the hooded beams of the ambulances shining into the underground entrance.

He pulled air as deep within his lungs as he could, and with that air came a fresh thought, the thought that Mrs Alford might actually have been waiting at home for Beau all this time.

That was it. With an almighty tug, he set himself free, his collar breaking and falling to the floor with a clatter.

He bounded on regardless. He was still Peggy's best boy, but from that moment, he had no evidence left to prove it.

22

Beau lay across the front step, resting, but not sleeping.

He felt sore, bruised. The pads of his feet, the joints of his legs, his ribs and neck, he felt them all, a ringing discomfort that made his entire body throb. It was nothing compared to the pain he felt in his gut whenever he thought of Mr and Mrs Alford.

The house had remained empty ever since his arrival home hours before. Lifeless. The only sound came from the high street, where horns still blared and buildings crumbled.

Beau felt a rising sense of panic. Where was Mrs Alford? Was she out from the depths, safe, resting at a friend's, perhaps? Was she lying on a stretcher somewhere or in an ambulance like those poor people he'd been rescuing for the last few weeks?

The night passed slowly. The sky grew darker and darker, as did Beau's thoughts, but eventually the gloom began to fade and people started to pass by, their faces drained of colour or joy. There were no conversations between them, no one fussed or stroked him, and if they knew where Mrs Alford was, they showed no interest in telling him.

The only other soul who *was* prepared to converse with him was someone he usually had no time for whatsoever.

'What on earth happened to you?' asked Mabel, slinking round the corner as if she'd enjoyed a carefree night on the tiles.

'What do you mean?' Beau replied tentatively, wanting desperately to know if she'd seen their missing owner.

'Well, look at the state of you. You're greyer than normal, which is saying something, and you're lying around like a geriatric instead of the annoying, bouncy fool you normally are.'

She wore her usual look, somewhere between smug and irritable.

'Have you no idea what's been going on?' Beau asked, incredulous.

'No,' Mabel replied, stretching blissfully, her eyes rolling back deliriously with the pleasure. 'Some of us have had better things to do. Some of us have been sampling the delights to be found on Wandsworth Common.' She looked close to sleep, so full was her belly.

'Then you didn't see the bomb? Or hear it?'

She shrugged as if to say, *Bombs are so passé these days*, which incensed Beau further.

'Is that it?' he barked. 'Is that the extent of your interest?'

'What do you want from me? A round of applause because you sniffed something out again?'

'Mr Alford is dead,' Beau replied, bluntly. 'Gone. And Mrs Alford? Well, I don't know, but a bomb exploded on the high street right above where she was sheltering. She hasn't come home.'

'Oh, you do like a drama, don't you? They're probably both still down in the tunnel, waiting for it all to pass.'

Beau looked at her in disgust. 'No, they aren't!' he roared. 'I'm not making this up. I watched Mr Alford, watched as they dragged his body away. There was a bomb, huge, it was. Like they'd dug up Hell and dropped it on our ruddy heads. It took Mr Alford with it, this huge hole that crumbled and pulled him down so deep that I couldn't get to him. I tried, I really did, but—'

Now he had Mabel's attention, though she still wore her haughty look of superiority.

'And there was no way he was still breathing?'

'Not a chance,' Beau said mournfully. 'I'd have smelled it if he was. He's gone, Mabel, and now I'm worried Mrs Alford has too.'

'Because . . .'

'Because the bomb burst a load of pipes above the shelter, didn't it? Gas and water, I heard them say.'

Mabel looked around her, could still see shocked folk stumbling by, dishevelled and weeping. 'Doesn't mean she's dead though, does it? I mean, look, people are still coming home now.'

'Then where is she? Because I looked for her underground. It was awful. The smell – it was like nothing I've ever come across. The tunnel had collapsed. I tried to get past it, dig my way through, but it wasn't just mud, it was concrete and steel and timber. It was ripping my paws to bits.' He tried to show

Mabel but as usual she wasn't interested. Her gaze was fixed in the direction of the station, the only way Mrs Alford would come back.

'Well, you mustn't panic, you fool.' Though Mabel didn't sound half as confident now. 'She'll be back. We must simply be patient. Now, do as I do.' And she jumped onto the front wall, stretching every vertebra up the length of her spine, before allowing herself to lie on the bricks.

Beau could not, and would not do the same. The adrenalin coursed in him too thickly for that. Instead he paced painfully, feeling crosser by the second. How could she be so disinterested, so dismissive, so completely and totally lacking in any kind of feeling for the poor Alfords? All she could do was lie there and sleep off her rodent banquet.

But what Beau didn't know from his vantage point was that Mabel's eyes were very much open. Open and fearful.

23

Mrs Alford did not come home. Not that morning or throughout the rest of the day.

Beau stewed in his anxiety. He tried, desperately, to be positive, to find reasons why she could have been delayed: that she'd only just been dug free, that she'd had to have minor wounds dressed, but none of them stuck for more than a moment. None of them could overpower the nagging, increasing certainty that something truly awful had happened to not just one of his owners, but both.

He wasn't anxious for himself. There was still a part of him that was and always would be a street dog. Yes, he'd had a blissful year living like a canine king with the Alfords, but if he had to return to the alleys and bins, then so be it. No, his fear, his sadness, his utter heartbreak was reserved purely for Peggy.

'How is she going to cope if it *has* happened?' he said out loud, on more than one occasion, not that Mabel ever replied. 'It's so unfair. She doesn't deserve this, and I don't think Aunt Sylvie can give her the care and love she needs. Her or Wilf.'

Finally, Mabel replied with a sigh. 'You've never even met the woman . . .'

'No, but I've heard Peggy's letters, haven't I? It's as much about what's written between the lines as well as on them. You must have heard the same things I did?

He waited for an answer, but it didn't come. What *did* come instead was a stocky woman in a housecoat and headscarf. Her tights were wrinkled, like they were sliding down her legs after the most exhausting of nights. But Beau's eyes were on the simple bunch of flowers she carried in her hands. They were small, insignificant, picked from an autumn garden, but tucked into their midst was a square piece of card, with a few words written untidily on it. As the woman neared the front step, Beau skittered away and watched instead from a distance, seeing emotion scratched deeply into the woman's forehead as she placed the posy on the doorstep. After dropping her head and mumbling something to herself, she wiped away a tear, and walked on.

Once she'd departed, Beau scampered back, desperate to work out what was written on the card. He nudged at it with his nose, then each of his front paws, but neither approach was successful.

'Oh for pity's sake,' huffed Mabel, finally on her feet, 'allow the brains through, will you?' And with a single, dextrous bat of her right paw, the piece of card slid effortlessly to the floor.

'What does it say then?' asked Beau impatiently.

Mabel looked slightly sheepish. 'Well, it's probably wishing Mrs Alford a happy birthday.'

Beau wasn't buying that.

'But the woman was crying. Who cries when they leave a birthday present for someone?'

'Maybe they're close friends, I don't know.'

'Rubbish! And besides, it was her birthday in the summer. Mr Alford tried to bake that cake.' Their argument was interrupted when a second couple shuffled up to the gate, pausing when they saw the flowers and card. Beau shuffled to the corner of the yard. Mabel did not.

'Oh, Henry,' the woman gasped. 'Look. That's the Alfords' house. And look what the card says.'

'I ain't got me glasses, Betty, whassit say?'

The woman leaned over, her bones almost creaking with the effort.

'Oh Lord,' she gasped. '*RIP*, it says. *You were a lovely couple.* Oh, Henry, that's awful, ain't it?'

'Terrible,' replied Henry solemnly as he spotted Mabel for the first time. ''Ere, in't this their cat?'

'Oh it is,' Betty said. 'And their dog there. Oh, Henry. The animals, they're all on their own.' She looked to her husband, her eyes silently saying something which Henry did not like.

'No,' he snapped, taking her wife's arm quickly. 'No, no, no, no, no!'

'But, Henry, look. They're all on their own. Who'll look after 'em?'

'A neighbour will take 'em in. Or family.'

'What if they don't have family?'

'Then there's the pound, in't there? They are not coming with us, we can 'ardly feed ourselves.'

As rejections went, it was pretty emphatic, and as Henry tugged his protesting wife on down the street, Mabel wished them well with the most venomous of hisses. 'I'd rather live rough than sleep on their sofa,' she declared, though Beau wasn't listening. He could only think of the pain that pulsed through him. He wanted to howl and cry.

'What are you two doing at the front?' another voice suddenly asked. 'I've been waiting for you round the back.' It was Bomber, but he was not his usual military-smart self. There was a ruffle to his feathers, like a bed that hadn't been made, and he was strutting, though not with pride. He looked on edge.

'Waiting for our humans,' replied Beau.

'Same here! We were due on a train at seven-thirty this morning. Training run, longest yet. But my people haven't come back all day. Most unlike them.'

'Where did they go?' Beau feared the answer but he had to ask.

'Underground station, last night, as per normal – they're always back pronto, soon as the siren sounds. But today? Not a sign of them. I have to say I'm not happy about it. Barely slept a wink, what with all the bombing last night, so I need today's flight to work out the cricks in my wings.'

'You'll have a long wait,' said Mabel, not an ounce of sympathy in her voice.

'Why's that?'

'Because apparently a bomb landed above the underground station. Broke all the gas and water pipes. The tunnel beneath flooded. Lots of people didn't make it out.'

Bomber looked shocked, his beak dropping open as he looked to Beau. 'Is this true?'

'It is. The Alfords, well, Mrs Alford, she was underground when it hit.'

'And Mr Alford?'

'He was above with me. But he didn't survive either.'

'So they're both . . .'

'Dead,' replied Mabel. 'Yes. Which is bad news for everyone involved.'

Her tone infuriated Beau again.

'It's not bad news,' he insisted, crossly. 'It's shocking. Awful. The worst. Because a hundred miles away, two children are now orphans. ORPHANS. And they don't even know it yet.'

Mabel said nothing, her head turned away.

'So my people . . . do you think . . . that they're . . . you know?' asked Bomber.

'I honestly don't know,' Beau replied. 'But if they're not back yet . . .'

Bomber gulped, before remembering who he was. He was Bomber, soldier-in-training, spy-in-waiting, and he sent a ripple through his feathers, which corrected some of them, before engaging them to their maximum span, taking off effortlessly.

'I'll be back,' he said. 'I just need to see this with my own eyes.'

Beau watched him as he cut the sky in two. There was a grace to his movements, an effortlessness, but more importantly, there was speed, velocity and guile. So much so that no sooner had he disappeared from sight than he seemed to reappear, settling on the wall.

'Oh,' he replied. 'Well, that doesn't look good. In fact, it looks blooming awful.'

'Are people still being brought out from down below?'

Bomber nodded sadly. 'They are, but not on their feet. On stretchers, covered in sheets.'

'I'm really sorry, Bomber,' Beau said. 'If your people are gone as well, then what are you going to do?'

Bomber slumped slightly, little pride in his chest for once. 'I've no idea. I was going to ask you the same thing.'

Beau felt Bomber's enquiring eyes on him, felt Mabel's too (though she tried to be sly about it) and knew instantly what his answer was.

He needed a deep breath before declaring it. Because one of the others was going to laugh at him, and he knew exactly which one it would be.

24

'I'm going to find Peggy,' Beau declared. The words did not sound at all silly once they were out there. 'She's going to need me. Just like I needed her.'

Mabel didn't laugh but didn't hesitate either in letting her feelings be known.

'Ridiculous,' she crowed. 'Ri-dic-U-LOUS.'

'Why? Why is it ridiculous?' He had the bit between his teeth now. He wasn't afraid of standing his ground.

'Because you're a dog.'

'And?'

'And what? That's every answer you could possibly need.'

'No, it isn't.'

'Yes, it is. You can't feed yourself. Or walk yourself. You can barely work out where your own backside is to lick it without a human pointing your nose in the right direction. So how do you think you can possibly track down Peggy when she's a hundred miles away? She'll be an old woman before you sniff her out.'

Beau was incensed. 'That's not true. I've been looking after myself most of my life. And I know exactly where she's living. Right by Anvil Point lighthouse.'

'Which is where?'

'On the coast, obviously.'

'Which coast?'

'The one on the sea.'

'In which town?'

'The one Sylvie lives in.' Beau could feel his exasperation rising. There was nothing wrong with his plan, or at least with its aspirations, even if the finer details needed a little fleshing out.

'Oh, forgive me,' sneered Mabel. 'That makes *all* the difference. You can of course just wander around every seaside town in the whole of the country, asking everyone, in your best human voice, "Excuse me, could you possibly point me in the direction of Aunt Sylvie's house? You know the one, it's by the lighthouse."'

'Sarcasm will get you nowhere,' Beau argued back.

'Further than being a stupid, ignorant dog will.'

On it went, barbs and derision slung back and forth. It was fortunate then, as Beau and Mabel circled each other, claws sharpening, that Bomber was there to put the pin safely back in the grenade.

'Anvil Point?' he mused, before his eyes widened suddenly. 'Anvil point! ANVIL POINT!!!'

Mabel glanced in his direction. 'That bird is as equally dense as you are,' she sneered. 'Though he would undoubtedly taste better.'

Beau didn't care about either of their gastronomic qualities. All he knew was that Bomber clearly wanted to tell him something.

'What about it, Bomber?' he asked.

'Well, I know it, don't I? Flew back from there, just the other week.'

'So, you know where it is? And what the town's called?'

'Course. It's a fair old distance. Especially for a dog.'

'Funny name for a seaside resort,' Mabel sneered again.

'That's not what it's called,' Bomber said. Mabel's sarcasm seemed to merely slide off him. 'It's just a fact. The town it's near is . . .'

Beau waited nervously. Mabel laughed ironically. 'Come on, genius, tell us.'

'It's on the tip of my tongue, isn't it? Big place. By the sea. Blooming big beach.'

'Well, that narrows it down . . .' Mabel was *loving* this.

'Come on . . .' Beau pleaded. Bomber was all he had right now.

'Starts with a B.'

'Bombay?' Mabel laughed. 'Bangkok? Berlin?'

But Mabel's jesting fell apart when Bomber fixed her with a hard stare. 'Don't be ridiculous,' he scolded. 'EVERYONE knows Berlin is nowhere near the sea.' His eyes lit up suddenly. 'Bournemouth! It's near Bournemouth. Well, that's where you'd need to get to first.'

'Bournemouth,' Beau replied with a knowing smile, though of course he was relying entirely on Bomber's intel. 'Of course.'

'That's where the train dropped us. Then we had to go further south on a bus and across the estuary on a ferry. From there, it wasn't too far, past a place called Swanage.'

Bomber looked delighted with himself. No wonder he was a super soldier in waiting.

Mabel, on the other hand, was feeling smug for a different reason. 'You remembering all of this, are you, dog?' she sneered.

'Course I am,' replied Beau.

'And you really think you can find your way to Peggy on your own?'

'Who said anything about him going on his own?' interjected Bomber.

'Me, because who wants to spend more than a couple of minutes in his company, never mind days?'

'Well, there's me for starters,' cooed Bomber.

'You?' both Mabel and Beau said together.

Mabel chuckled, but Beau stared at the bird in surprise.

'You'd come with me?' he said. 'To show me the way?'

'Why not?'

'Well, because you're in training, waiting for your big call up. Your first mission.'

Bomber sighed deeply and looked towards his empty house. 'Yes, well, it doesn't look like that's going to happen any time soon. Not with my people . . . well, gone.'

'But what if the army were to turn up while you were away?'

Mabel rolled onto her back now, howling with laughter. 'Oh stop it,' she guffawed, 'this is hurting, it's so funny.'

But her plan to humiliate them backfired. It galvanised

Bomber, pushing his chest out so far it looked like he was hiding an egg under his feathers.

'Then they'd simply have to wait,' he replied. 'Just like I have all this time. I'm in prime physical condition with a mind so sharp it could cut iron. If I didn't come to the aid of a comrade in need, then what sort of soldier would I be?'

'A sensible one,' roared Mabel. 'You two won't last five minutes out there.'

'Rubbish,' replied Beau. 'I've spent practically the whole of my life on the streets.'

'Smells like it,' Mabel said.

'And as for me,' said Bomber, 'well, I've seen more of this country and its dangers than you ever will. I'm a coiled spring, a fighting machine.'

'You're a rat with wings,' Mabel replied. 'And him?' She tipped her head at Beau, 'well . . . he's just a rat. Good luck to you, I say.'

'So you're not coming with us?' Beau asked, tentatively.

'Ha! Are you kidding me? Why would I do that?'

'To comfort your Wilf. Your Wilf, who loves you.'

Mabel shifted uncomfortably, lacking her usual poise or swagger. 'The boy hasn't sent me so much as a postcard, never mind the love letters you've had. He clearly doesn't even remember I'm alive.'

'Course he does. He needs you. Especially now that his parents are gone.'

'Nonsense. He needs me as much as . . . well, as I need

him.' There was undoubtedly a whiff of petulance about what she was saying. 'So I'll be staying here, where there's rats on tap and everyone knows I'm boss.'

Beau was disappointed in her, and saddened for Wilf, but knowing her stubbornness, he shrugged and made to leave.

'Well, we'll be off then,' he declared. 'If you're ready, Bomber?'

'I was born ready,' the pigeon replied, already strutting.

But as they made their first, assertive steps, they were halted momentarily by one final comment from Mabel.

'You do know it's going to be difficult, don't you? It's not the end of the street you're talking about.'

Both Beau and Bomber shrugged it off.

'So how far are you prepared to go?' Mabel shouted. 'How long will you keep looking for two small children?'

'Do you really need to ask?' Beau said, with one last look over his shoulder. 'This is Peggy we're talking about. And Wilf too. So I'll keep looking until the road ends. It's as simple as that.'

25

They didn't pause when they hit Balham High Road.

The crumpled remains of the bus had been hoisted somehow from the crater, but looked even scarier now, battered as it was. Beau felt his insides lurch and tasted acid in his mouth. He swallowed it down successfully, but was helpless to the emotion that was brimming inside.

'Don't be filling your head with thoughts of last night, soldier,' Bomber cooed as he landed beside him. 'Only thing you need to be thinking of now is the road in front of you. That, and your Peggy.'

Beau knew he was right. 'It's just a shame Mabel didn't feel the same way.'

Bomber took to the skies, as if worried that the mere mention of her name would summon her to pounce. 'Never yet met a cat that I liked or trusted. Can't see that changing any time soon, either. She had a choice. She was either with us or against us. And I don't see her now, do you?'

Beau shook his head.

'Well, then. Keep your eyes on the prize, which is that lighthouse. It's out there, over the horizon. Find Anvil Point and we win this battle.'

These were fine words. Inspiring, and despite the pain he

117

felt, Beau forced himself to look away from the carnage, in the direction of Clapham Junction and the train to Bournemouth, which Bomber had told him about. With a deep breath, he trotted on, Bomber hovering and dipping, as if testing his engines.

For the next twenty minutes, they weaved through the crowds of people as they went about their business, boarding-up smashed windows and door frames. Long snakes of dusty-faced, headscarved women passed bricks and rubble along their lengths, stacking them high on a cart ready to be pulled by a huge shire horse.

Beau nodded in respect and appreciation at the beast, who acknowledged him back with a sigh which seemed to suggest that all of this devastation could so easily have been avoided.

It was a look that stayed with Beau.

'We *are* heading in the right direction, aren't we?' he asked Bomber, as the pair of them hit Clapham Common. It stretched out as far as the eye could see.

'Follow me, follow me, this way,' sang Bomber.

Time passed, the ink of the sky turning red, violet, indigo then black as they crossed the park.

'You hungry?' Beau asked Bomber.

'No,' the bird insisted without hesitation. 'A fighting machine, me. Trained to exist on my wits alone.'

Beau *was* hungry, but he tried not to think about anything other than reaching Clapham Junction station. Until he saw an innocuous shop front on the high street, its lights dimmed, but still exuding an overwhelmingly delicious smell.

'That's salt,' barked Beau. 'Vinegar too.' He steered left immediately, nose to the ground. 'And batter. Bloomin' chip shop, it must be!'

'Maybe, but it's also shut,' replied Bomber. 'As the train station will be if we don't push on.'

But Beau was deaf to his warning.

'Not yet, Bomber. I mean, we need to eat, don't we? And where there's a chip shop, there's a bin, and where there's a bin, there's scraps.'

'Scraps?'

'Yes, scraps. Bits of batter. All golden and crunchy. Stuck to the occasional chip.'

Beau's tail was circling so excitedly it looked like he may take off at any second. He didn't though, choosing instead to skitter down an alleyway next to the shop.

'Bingo!' he yelled, as he found a large metal dustbin, which he expertly barged over, the lid rolling to the floor with a satisfyingly loud clang.

And there it was, his bounty, wrapped clumsily in newspaper.

Beau pushed his muzzle deep inside, unearthing not only a mound of golden batter, but several handfuls of chips *and* a crispy fish tail.

'Here,' he said, licking his already greasy muzzle. 'Try a bit of this, Bomber. Heaven.'

The bird wasn't completely convinced, he still had half a mind on the late hour and the chances of them catching a train, but after a few pecks, he knew that this was a taste sensation he couldn't refuse.

'Do you think we should save some?' Beau asked after a few more greedy gulps. 'You know, we don't know where the next meal is coming from, do we?'

'Excellent thinking. I'll make a soldier of you yet.' And the two of them set about closing the bundle back up with beaks and paws, before Beau clamped it in his jaws.

Normally, it would take a lot for the dog to resist such a delicious prize, but not tonight. He was a soldier. And he bounded along the pavement to prove it. He knew that Peggy was still a long, long way away, but every step took him closer, which in turn made him feel stronger. He moved with such speed, that even Bomber had to find a new gear to keep up with him.

'Nearly there, Bomb,' he mouthed through the newspaper. 'We'll be on the train in no time.' And he believed it too, though once they reached the entrance of the station, he felt a drop in his stomach that had little to do with the greasy chips he'd devoured.

The place was empty. Deserted. No sound of trains straining to be released or whistles being blown. There wasn't a single smell about the place that suggested a living soul remained on site.

'Oh,' said Beau, dropping the bundle.

'I did tell you it was late,' Bomber sighed, landing on his back. 'Looks like we've missed the last one.'

'So what do we do now?'

'Well, unless you fancy walking . . .' Bomber flexed his wings as if to prove that it would be no problem to him, '. . . then we should find you somewhere to rest.'

'And what about you?'

'Soldiers never sleep,' the pigeon replied, almost indignantly. 'Or if we do, it's with one eye open. You need to be fresh. I'll keep watch.'

Beau could've offered to take watch himself, but he knew it would be a fruitless exercise. Bomber had waited for this, this moment, this adventure, and to take it from him seemed almost cruel. And besides, it was late, his aching limbs told him so. The only problem they faced was finding a spot where they could rest peacefully.

Every store cupboard was padlocked, as was the ticket office, and as for the platforms themselves? They had transformed into wind tunnels that would offer no respite whatsoever.

All they could do in the end was huddle beneath the stairwell on platform fifteen, the steps serving as a partial windbreak. The concrete beneath Beau was cold and damp, but he didn't care. He took solace from a few more chips, before leaving the newspaper bundle by his midriff. It would be a reassuring smell to wake up to.

Bomber chose a wooden strut on the stairwell, where he perched, head rotating almost like a lighthouse as he surveyed the horizon for threats and danger.

The boredom of his mission soon took hold of him however, and his eyelids began to sag, until first his right eye, and then his left closed.

But as the two intrepid animals slept, the platform around them awoke, as in the shadows, one by one, a sea of narrow eyes opened, all of them fixed menacingly on Beau.

It took only minutes for the dog and his parcel to have a hundred greedy admirers, and slowly, stealthily, they moved in on the prize.

26

It was a delicious dream.

Beau was covered in a thick, furry blanket which seemed to almost massage him. A moving, vibrating cover that pressed and eased his limbs, stiff from walking.

But dreams are unpredictable things, and the brain complex. For just as the blanket seemed to be heaven-sent, it changed beyond measure.

It grew teeth, which one by one, started to tease at Beau's fur. He felt them on his rump, behind his ears, but especially on his midriff. The teeth seemed to sharpen. A nip at first, then a pull, followed by what can only be described as a bite. Beau stiffened, his front right paw flicking at the blanket, which only made it fight back harder and in more places. His eyes flew open, straining into the deathly gloom.

'What's that?' he said groggily, twitching his front legs, only for the pain to intensify. 'Get off, will you?'

But the biting escalated, sending Beau into a shocked frenzy.

He leaped to his feet, but the blanket held on, swaying with his every movement, refusing point-blank to be thrown to the floor.

Beau's eyes widened, his senses gathering, as he realised

what the blanket actually was. An army of dirty, hungry rats, senses aroused by the greasy newspaper of cold chips and scraps. The bundle was swarming with them still as they ripped and tore at the paper, swallowing its oily print instead of discarding it.

But some had decided that Beau was far tastier, and no matter how quickly he shook his limbs, they were determined not to let go of their prey.

'Get off, get off. Help, help!' he squealed, his limbs on fire, his senses overloaded.

In time of war, a soldier needs a comrade. And Beau had one. Down from the beam above tore Bomber, wings dipped, beak pushed forward as he dove.

This was what he had been bred to do: to fight evil.

But as he landed on top of the closest rat, he realised that his strategy was all wrong. It's a reckless soldier who dashes in. The clever ones, the ones who come through unscathed, alive, are the ones who strategise, evaluating their own strengths and weaknesses against those of their opponents. This was not a battle that Bomber could win at close quarters. His power would only come if he fought from range. Bomber by name, bomber by nature.

But he learned this the hard way. He did manage to remove the first rat's jaws from Beau's back, but this awoke the attention of the others around him. And when they spotted that a *bird* was on the menu, it didn't take long for a clutch of them to launch themselves in Bomber's direction, all of them falling short bar one, who clipped Bomber's right wing, sending him nosediving to the floor, where he rolled, tucking his head artfully beneath his wing on impact.

Such a crash drew further interest from a new wave of rats, who scampered in his direction, leaping skywards as Bomber pulled himself towards the rafters. One managed to make significant contact, front teeth locking onto the tips of Bomber's tailfeathers.

The pigeon knew nothing of it until he felt himself falling, no matter how hard he pounded his wings. He knew he had seconds, if that. All he could do was use his warrior instinct, and he kicked hard with his sharp, taloned feet, feeling his altitude soar as the rat tumbled to the floor, landing with a crack, a single feather still clamped between its front teeth.

There was no time for celebration though. Firstly, he needed to adjust to his tail now being a feather lighter, and then he must return to his original mission. Beau had tried to remain on his feet, writhing and swinging his body in every direction he could without falling onto the tracks, but the weight of the rats, and the pain they were inflicting on him soon saw him reduced to a shuddering wreck who had no answer to the ceaseless attack.

Bomber circled above, looking for any sign of weakness in their formation, but whichever angle he peered down from, he saw nothing. He tried divebombing, shrieking as he went, but the rats were not intimidated. In fact they barely seemed to acknowledge he was there.

He tried to play them at their own game: landing on their backs and sinking his beak deep into their skin, but the risk was simply too high. By staying still for longer than a second, he saw attacks from all sides, and whilst he was made of tough stuff, he knew he couldn't fight off an entire army.

All he could do was circle from above, threatening impotently with the occasional halfhearted divebomb, as Beau was besieged.

But just as Bomber thought the campaign might be over before it had truly begun, there came an unexpected rearguard action, as from the blackness stormed a new weapon – a whirlwind, a maelstrom of fur and hissing that tore across the platform, before throwing itself deep into the middle of the throng. Within seconds, the teeming blanket started to unravel and disperse, with rats flying to all corners of the platform at a terrifying rate. Seeing an opportunity, Bomber began a new advance of his own, picking out rats at the periphery, diving with such speed and ferocity that it startled them, before they sprinted back to the shadows.

Again and again he spiralled, up and down, nipping at backs, whilst keeping half an eye on Beau, who was now fighting back himself.

Bomber had never seen this side of Beau before: the street dog, the stray, the one who had survived so long on scraps and beds beside dustbins, but as Beau bared his teeth and growled in resistance, it was impossible not to be impressed, and the fightback continued.

The new arrival continued to terrorise the rats, hissing and scratching, throwing them mercilessly onto the tracks, and in between attacks of his own, Bomber strained to get a better view of them, not believing his eyes when finally they slowed long enough to reveal their identity.

'Mabel!' Bomber cried, not knowing whether to laugh or die of shock. Where on earth had she come from? And more to the point, why on earth was she here?

27

Minutes later the trio stood alone on the platform. Wheezing, tired and victorious.

'Mabel?' Beau said, so breathless and bewildered that he thought he was hallucinating. 'It's not you, is it?'

'No. Of course not,' she replied. 'It's Adolf Hitler.'

Beau fell to the floor in exhaustion. Her sarcasm wasn't a surprise, but the fact that she was now in front of him definitely was.

'I don't understand. What are you doing here?'

'Doing? I'm doing what I always knew I'd have to do. Saving your behinds, that's what. And you're welcome, by the way. Don't even mention it.'

'But I thought . . . well . . . I thought you weren't interested in helping?'

'I'm not. But at the same time, I'm not *completely* evil . . .'

Beau and Bomber exchanged a dubious look.

'I just realised, as I relaxed and enjoyed my new life of freedom, that I couldn't allow you to struggle on your own. Without me . . . well, it's clear after this debacle, that you can't possibly succeed without me.'

She looked deep into Beau's eyes. He knew what she was doing. She was daring him to disagree so she could throw her heroics straight back into his face. And the problem was, she had him over a barrel. Because on this occasion it was true. Without her, they would've been well and truly stuffed. That didn't mean that he believed her reasoning though.

'Well, we're grateful, aren't we, Bomb?' Beau conceded.

Bomber nodded but tried to disguise it as pecking at a rogue crumb.

'But you've done your job now, you've bailed us out. So there's no need to stick around. We won't be making the same mistake again.'

'We most certainly won't,' added Bomber emphatically. 'So bye-bye. All the best.'

Mabel took this as her cue to sit on the platform and sigh theatrically.

'Oh, I couldn't possibly leave you like that. You see, I've been thinking, with the parents . . . gone, I'm the closest thing to an adult you have, so I feel it's my duty to deliver you safely to those poor, poor children.'

Mabel was a cat, and as Beau knew only too well, they were scheming, devious and stubborn creatures. Her reasons for being here didn't add up. But Beau decided that the best thing for now was to say as little as possible, until he could work out what she was up to.

'All right then,' he said, before turning his attention to his front legs, inspecting himself for bites and cuts (of which, he knew, he had many).

'All right, what?' Mabel replied, confused. Bomber shot Beau a look which said the same thing.

'You can come,' he said, not looking up. 'Safety in numbers and all that.'

Bomber's expression went from confused to downright indignant. 'Er, hang on,' he interjected. 'Don't I get a say in this? I am in effect, the senior officer here.'

'I know, but it's no good having the finest general in the world if there are too few troops to carry out the orders, is it?' Beau said.

Bomber was slightly seduced by these words, he couldn't lie, but at the same time, he dragged Beau to one side for a private conflab.

'What are you playing at?' he mouthed.

'It's all right,' Beau replied, making sure Mabel couldn't overhear. 'That cat loves conflict even more than the Nazis. Stand up to her and she'll make your life a misery. Ignore her and it drives her potty.'

'I'm not so sure.'

'Trust me, Bomb, I've lived with her for a year, and fighting and bullying are her reasons for living. If we keep it low key for long enough she'll get angry, then bored. I give it six hours max before she decides she's had enough and turns for home.'

Bomber sighed. 'And in the meantime, I'm still the commanding officer?'

'You are.'

'Hmmmm. Then we proceed as planned. Rest. Wait for

the train. If we're lucky we will be in Bournemouth by the afternoon.'

That suited Beau just fine, though he doubted he would sleep again. Not just because of the threat of the rats, but also the pain that was starting to shoot through his many nicks and bites.

All he wanted was for dawn to creep on quickly, and for the train to eat up the miles to the coast. Peggy needed him and that was the only thing he could think about.

28

It was still rather dark when the station started to fill up; bleary-eyed passengers lining the platform, warming their fingers on cigarettes that intermittently lit the gloom.

Beau stayed tucked away beneath the staircase. People seemed tolerant of Mabel strolling along the platform, in fact, she was collecting strokes and affection as she paraded herself along its entire length. But Beau knew he'd be regarded as a stray and probably carted off to the pound, where he knew what would happen to him. The same that had happened to so many dogs at the start of the war.

'Are we definitely on the right platform?' he whispered to Bomber, still perched above him.

'We are. I heard the gent by the ticket hall tell three different people. Be patient, soldier. We'll be on the way soon.'

Ten minutes later they heard the unmistakable clamour of a train approaching: a leg-shaking vibration in the floor, growing stronger and louder, until the train's cab hoved into view, belching thick clouds into the air.

'BOURNEMOUTH!' yelled a man in a peaked cap and matching blue suit, though how he managed to make himself heard against the racket of the train was a complete mystery.

Beau braced himself to stand.

'Not yet,' said Bomber landing beside him. 'Wait for it. Let the people on first. Then we need to dash for the end of the train, there'll be cargo carriages there we can hide in, away from prying eyes. And you never know, we may make it onboard without that cat noticing.'

Beau did as instructed. He couldn't risk not scrabbling onboard this train. There may be others that followed later, but to his mind it had to be *this* one. He needed to be with Peggy, to calm her, to save her like she'd rescued him. So ignoring the red-hot pokers of pain that stung his skin, he braced, not moving an inch until Bomber finally gave the order, with a single: 'Chaaaaarge!'

They raced along the platform, bullet fast, ignoring the wide eyes of passengers already seated onboard. Beau followed the path set by Bomber, who sliced the air with his beak.

If the dog needed any extra motivation it soon came in the shape of Mabel, bounding beside him effortlessly, a leer on her face as she pushed her nose into the lead. Beau responded, he wasn't going to let her board first, not a chance, and so a race began. They hared past first class, not slowing as the standard carriages followed. But this was a sprint with only one victor, and as the final carriages whipped past, one of them adorned with bright circus-like lettering, Beau had reestablished a comfortable lead.

'Open door, next carriage,' Bomber cried from above.

Beau barked his approval, and steered left before jumping

onboard, not landing until all four legs were safely inside. Mabel followed suit with a similar energy before Bomber soared in, hitting the brakes in the most graceful fashion, landing lightly on a huge brown sack.

'Excellent work, troops,' he cooed. 'Nobody suspected a thing.'

But as famous last words go, these were poor ones.

''Ere, Jack. Did you see that?' A thick cockney voice bellowed from the platform.

'See what, Terry?'

The animals dashed deep into the shadows, crouching behind boxes and sacks.

'I could've sworn I saw a dog, a cat and a sparrow get on carriage C.'

Beau saw Bomber bristle at being so heinously mistaken for a sparrow.

'Bit early to have the hip flask out, ain't it, Tel? Din't you have enough to drink down the Feathers last night?'

'I'm telling you, Jack, I saw what I saw.'

They heard the man laugh, then tell the other one to check the carriage anyway, before hearing footsteps, and a groan as Terry heaved himself onboard.

'Cheeky swine,' he breathed. 'He had way more pints than me.'

The footsteps continued, clumsy and heavy. Beau and Mabel pushed themselves deeper into the shadows. They heard the strike of a match and Beau feared the worst. If the man lit a lantern then it would be almost impossible for them to stay hidden. The gloom was their only ally.

Beau looked up to the ceiling for Bomber: for any kind of sign. Would the bird tell them to charge and knock the man off balance before running for it? Or did the commanding officer have a different plan? But the pigeon was nowhere to be seen. Was camouflage another of his many military skills?

Beau held his breath as he heard a tut and a sigh, then another match being lit. The first must have blown out. Maybe luck was on their side.

But then the dog smelled something unexpected. The sweet aroma of tobacco burning, then a long exhalation as Terry puffed the smoke out into the stale air of the carriage. He wasn't lighting a lantern after all, only his pipe.

Suddenly there came the ear-piercing shrill of a whistle blowing from the platform outside. The train was ready to depart.

''old on, 'old on,' Terry gasped through his pipe, 'I'm still onboard 'ere, I am!' and he scampered to the door, almost thrown off balance as the train lurched forward once, then twice.

Oh no, thought Beau. The last thing they needed was the man to remain a stowaway like them. Should he dash forward and give Terry a helpful push? Just enough to see him out of the door? He watched uncertainly, willing the man on as he stumbled, crouched and finally found the balance needed to jump clumsily down to the platform, just as the train found the start of its jerking rhythm. Beau couldn't help dashing to poke his head through the gap in the sliding door to check the man hadn't done himself a terrible mischief. Mabel, never one to miss out, did the same, as did Bomber.

And there Terry was, sitting on the platform, rubbing at a very sore ankle, his pipe shattered beside him. He was in some pain, that was clear, but it didn't stop him from looking up and finally clocking the animals that he knew he'd seen before.

''Ere Jack!!' he bellowed. 'Look, look I told ya, din't I? Exactly as I said!'

But his protestations fell on deaf ears.

'I'm a pigeon, you fool!' squawked Bomber defiantly, but his voice was lost to the lungs of the train as it pulled quickly away. They were on the move. And Bournemouth and Peggy were getting closer with every second.

29

The train took some getting used to.

Beau didn't have a lot in the way of expectations, having never been on one before, and it left a lot to be desired. The bumpiness was the first challenge. It was hard to put more than a few steps together without a sudden jolt making him weave like a drunkard. He had always prided himself on his balance, his agility. It had seen him wriggle from many a sticky situation while he lived masterless on the streets. *Maybe I've gone soft*, he thought to himself. Regular meals and nights in front of the fire had blunted him, made him, dare he say it ... domesticated? But as he thought that, he remembered the benefits of such a lifestyle. The comfort, the warmth, the connection, which led him straight back to thinking of Peggy and that returning knot deep in his gut.

'What do you think she's doing now?' he asked no one in particular. 'My Peggy.'

'If she has any sense, she's sleeping,' murmured Mabel.

'Sleeping? With everything that must be going on in her head? I doubt she'll sleep for weeks.' Worry filled Beau to the brim and he began to pace, tripping left and right, which delighted Mabel no end.

'Steady on, soldier,' barked Bomber sternly but

sympathetically. 'Worrying will get you nowhere. In fact, it will only hamper our progress. A good soldier is single-minded. Thinks only of the mission's objective, not the emotion that accompanies it.'

Beau was growing to like Bomber more and more; the bird was unspeakably brave and true, yet he did constantly seem to forget that Beau was not actually a soldier. He was a dog. A good dog, but definitely a dog.

Mabel, on the other hand, found it all simply baffling. 'You really are a crackpot, bird,' she sneered. 'A tasty crackpot, I'm sure, but a crackpot all the same.'

'And you're a cynic,' interjected Beau. 'A cynic who's free to leave whenever you choose.'

'But if I did that, I'd miss all the fun. Not to mention the opportunity to save your behinds again and again. I mean, who knows how many scrapes I'll have to dig you out of between here and the coast?'

Beau bit his tongue. To argue further would be to go against his own advice to Bomber. She was best ignored, and he managed to do that with his feathered friend's help.

'You know, it is possible that if we advance with speed and stealth, we may make it to Peggy before she even hears the news.'

This made Beau prick up his ears *and* his spirits.

'You think so?'

'I know so. Because let's face it: it was a terrible thing that happened. And no small explosion. Who knows how many actually died, but I think it's safe to say it was a lot. They will need to identify bodies, type up telegrams, and that's before they even work out where to send them.'

Beau drank this in thirstily.

'Then I'll run down to the driver's cab and shovel on coal myself,' he said.

'Really,' purred Mabel, 'I didn't realise you had opposable thumbs these days. Though I must say, if you do, you could have been burying your poos like I always have. Lazy beast.' And she closed her eyes, smugly.

It took every last bit of restraint Beau had not to bite back both verbally and physically, but fortunately he realised his energy would be better spent tending again to the many nicks that covered his body thanks to his rat friends back on the platform.

Even this essential job couldn't keep his mind from Peggy. He hung on grimly to the possibility that right now, she was asleep in bed, blissfully unaware of everything that had gone on back in Balham. It was reassuring in some small way, the bumps and vibrations of the carriage for the first time feeling mildly pleasant, comforting even, and Beau allowed them to ripple through his belly and into his legs, until they pulled and teased his eyelids lazily down.

He didn't sleep long, but he drifted dreamlessly in and out for a while, before stretching his legs as best he could in the cramped carriage, settling eventually on a crate that sat beside an open window.

The view outside was alien to him. He was a city dog, so to now be faced, even intermittently, with the sight of fields, and the occasional river, well, he didn't know whether to be fascinated or daunted.

'Not exactly like home, is it?' said Bomber, landing beside him.

'Where did all the sky come from?'

'Oh, it was always there. It was just hiding, like so many things in the city. It's so busy there, it has to fight to be seen.'

Beau stopped and contemplated that. 'What's it like . . . to fly in it?'

Bomber thought about it for a moment as he stared glassily out of the window.

'Powerful.'

'Powerful?' It wasn't the answer Beau was expecting.

'Powerful. I mean, look at the legs on me. I'm not built for speed when I'm on the floor like this. I'm a sitting target to predators like the moggy over there. But soon as my engines ignite and I'm off the ground? Well, it feels like nothing can keep up with me, never mind touch me. I can outsprint or outdistance anyone or anything. And that, soldier, is what power feels like.'

'Wow. Blimey.' Beau couldn't help but feel impressed and envious that he'd never experience it himself.

'It's not a surprise that they say this war may be won in the air. And that's why I'm a soldier. So I can do my bit.'

'Well, you're certainly doing that. And I'm grateful. I really am.'

'Steady now, private. I don't need praise,' Bomber said. 'Though if we are successful in our mission, then I wouldn't say no to a medal . . . as long as you don't prick me with the pin.'

Beau wagged his tail, though not for long as he remembered his own painful skin.

He tried to take his mind off it by focusing on the view as it raced by, slightly shrouded in the locomotive's bellowing smoke. The city of course was long gone, and even the towns that followed seemed to grow smaller with every passing mile. The thing Beau noticed more of though, was children. They seemed to punctuate the route, standing on embankments, waving innocently as the train tore past. It was wishful thinking, he knew, but every girl he spotted seemed to look like his Peggy. He'd double-take, then stare, barking on occasion when the similarities and the longing he had for her overwhelmed him.

There had been so few children in the city this past year, despite those returning from evacuation, that it took some getting used to, seeing them like this, and all of them so innocent, so happy, away from the rubble and toppled buildings of London.

If only Peggy could have remained untouched by war. But he was her hope and her future now, and nothing, *nothing*, could stop him from reaching her.

Or so he thought.

30

Having spent so much time (literally) licking his wounds, it wasn't long before Beau felt thirsty. With it came listlessness and also irritability, especially where Mabel was concerned.

'Will you LEAVE ME ALONE!' he barked after the cat had sought to wind him up for the umpteenth time, seemingly without drawing breath.

'You're touchy, aren't you?' Mabel purred, delirious that she had finally got under the mutt's skin.

'Little wonder, with you tormenting him all the time,' said Bomber. 'Hardly good for troop morale, is it?'

'He's not a soldier and I'm not bothered,' she replied, as dry as Beau's mouth. 'I'm just here for the sport.'

'I'm going to find some water,' Beau said, wincing in pain as he pushed himself to his feet. He started hunting and sniffing amongst the crates for something, anything he could drink.

'You'll not find anything in here, you fool,' she laughed, which made Beau search harder, then feel even more aggrieved when it turned out she was right.

'It's all right, Beau,' reassured Bomber. 'Give it time and we'll be stopping at the next station. Soon as we do, I'll check the coast is clear for you to look in the next carriage. You'll find some, I'm sure.'

Beau breathed deeply. He could feel Mabel's eyes on him, looking for a new angle from which to verbally attack, but fortunately, within minutes, he felt the brakes being applied and the train slowing.

'Told you,' said Bomber, himself relieved. 'Wait for my signal.' And he took off, through the gap in the carriage door.

Beau waited, realising he had no idea what the signal actually was, but it was too late to shout after his friend. Instead, he waited, coiled in the doorway, only jumping down when Bomber conducted a fly-by, yelling 'NOW!' as he passed.

The platform was quiet enough, any activity limited to the front of the train where passengers came and went. It was of no interest to Beau anyway. He simply wanted to go unnoticed, and squeezed silently through the smallest gap onto the next carriage, which was not dissimilar to the first: crates, boxes and sacks, stacked and piled high, but none of them yielding anything that would help him. There was no sign of Mabel though, so he had that to be grateful for if nothing else.

Back on the platform, he pushed his nose to the ground, but could not sense a drop of water anywhere.

The third carriage, however, was different. It held very different cargo. There were no sacks or boxes, just several suitcases covered in exotic stickers, a hanging rail holding a magnificent array of colourful costumes, whilst in the middle of the space stood a huge wooden crate.

It towered above Beau, and of course, he had a good sniff as he circled it slowly. What his nose found perplexed him: there was a slightly fishy aroma, but not one that he could identify, and it was only there fleetingly. It came and went, and it bothered him that he couldn't quite work it out.

'Nose letting you down, is it?'

Ugh, Mabel. She had one eye on the hanging rail and one on him. Fortunately, she seemed drawn to the clothes on show.

'You'd look lovely in this,' she scoffed, nodding at an elaborate headdress that looked like a mad mixture of feathers stolen from a variety of rare birds. It might have been murky dark in the carriage, but the colours still seemed to shine.

'You'll be eating it in a minute,' he replied sullenly. 'I mean, who wears things like that in the middle of a war?'

'Oh Beau, Beau, Beau, if only your eyes were as keen as that snout of yours. Were you not looking at the train as you ran to jump onboard it?'

'I was trying to keep up with Bomber, so why would I?'

'Because if you had, you'd have seen that this carriage is different to the others. It's special. It belongs to a different kind of passenger.'

'Right, and are you expecting me to guess who that is, because if you are, it's not a game I want to play.' And he made to walk away.

'It belongs to a mesmerist,' Mabel sighed, as if it were an everyday statement.

'A mesmer-what?'

'A mesmerist, you fool. A performer. Someone who can control your mind in the name of entertainment. You know, the kind you'd see at a circus.'

'Can't say I've ever been.' Beau really was on the verge of leaving now.

'This one happens to be called Koringa.'

'You're just making up words now,' Beau said. 'Because I know you can't read, so ha! I'm not falling for it.'

'It's true, you fool. I heard a woman telling her child as the train arrived at Clapham. And besides, I'm hurt by your words. I'm only trying to help.'

'As if,' huffed Beau.

'I am! Cats need water too, you know. Now, the woman also said the show involves animals.'

'What kind?'

'I don't know. But if it does, then they'll need water, just like us.'

'Well, I can't see any other animals.' Beau span round as if to make his point. He even called out 'Hello?' but got no response.

'Oh, for pity's sake,' spat Mabel. 'In the crate! If there's animals to be found, they're sure to be in the crate. And if the animals are in there, then the water will be too. Do I have to spoon-feed you every single thing in order to keep you alive? Why can't you smell it with that all-powerful nose of yours?'

Beau turned and faced the crate. Breathing in deeply, he felt an immediate sense of shame. There it was. Water.

He knew it now and took in the crate. It really was quite a size, and the height of it meant there was no chance of him seeing inside, even if perched on his rear legs. Mabel saw this as another opportunity to prove her superiority. With no type of run-up, with barely an arching of her back, she sprang skywards, and landed effortlessly on the top edge of the box, as if it were a high wire.

'What can you see?' Beau asked. He didn't care that she'd managed it now. All he wanted was a drink.

'Just a minute!' she hissed. 'It's even darker up here.' There was a pause as her eyes acclimatised. 'Well, the good news is, there's no lid on the crate.'

Beau was pleased about that, if there had been, there would be no way they could shift it between them. 'So. What's in there?'

'Be patient!'

So he was, and he waited, peering into the darkness, watching Mabel dip her head and upper body inside the crate without losing her balance. If he hadn't disliked her so much, he might have been impressed.

'It's strange,' she said. 'There's . . . bars, all the way across the top.'

'Bars? What do you mean?'

'Exactly that, you fool. Bars. Metal bars. And under the bars . . . There's water! I can see it. Masses of it. In fact, it's all water. There's a tank in here. A glass tank, I think, and it's full to the brim!'

Beau scrabbled up the side of the crate. Or at least he tried to. It was way too high for him to get any kind of purchase. He wondered how he could scale it to reach the bounty on offer, but as it turned out, he should've been thinking about something else. Like, why there was a huge tank of water sitting in the middle of a dingy train carriage. And even more importantly, what might be swimming inside it.

31

The situation was entirely to Mabel's liking.

What the dog wanted, more than anything, she had in abundance. A veritable lake of it.

All right, so she had no guarantees of its freshness, and it was too dark in there for her to inspect it properly, but he wanted it, and she had it, and that pleased her immeasurably.

All she had to do was lean over between one of the bars and take her fill, which she started to do. It was a bit of a mission to keep her balance whilst dipping her head between the bars, but she had no shortage of faith in her own ability, and as her tongue lapped at the water, she made sure Beau could hear just how delicious and life-giving it was.

But as she began to lap it up, something strange happened.

The water moved.

Not just ripples caused by her drinking, no, this was more than that, though she couldn't see what had caused it. She lifted her head, banging the bars in the process, which made her wobble momentarily. She stared at the water, thought she saw it sway again, then put it down to both an overactive imagination and too much time spent with an idiot dog.

'What you doing up there?' Beau called from below. 'And more importantly, how am I going to get any water?'

But as Mabel turned to tell him to hush, it came again, the movement. And this time it was no ripple, it was a wave, as something long and green and scaly broke the surface, moving with such speed and elasticity that it was a blur, before disappearing beneath the surface again.

'What's happening?' Beau called. 'Is there something inside?' He'd not seen it, but he could tell the cat was spooked.

'I don't know, but I'm getting dow—'

Mabel didn't finish her sentence. She couldn't, as without warning, the monster from the deep emerged for a second time: a wild, thrashing green limb, emerging and spraying water all over Beau.

He was too shocked to drink it, though not as shocked as when Mabel wobbled and fell with a splash beneath the surface.

'MABEL!' Beau yelped. She may not have been his friend, but he didn't wish that on her.

He tried again to scale the side of the crate, but even if his claws dug in once or twice, they wouldn't hold enough times to allow him to reach even halfway up.

He barked and whined and circled the crate several times, looking for something, anything, a way of allowing him to help. But there was nothing, and there was no sound from above now either, just an eerie silence, as the final droplets of water dribbled down the side of the wood.

'Bomber!' Beau shouted. 'BOMBER! COME QUICK! HELP!'

He was confused and downright terrified. Was Mabel all right? Was the thing hurting her? Holding her underwater or even worse . . .

He had to do something, and so he scratched again at the side of the crate, his claws finally catching as he clambered like a mountain goat. But as the apex approached and his chest tightened with the exertion, he felt a presence above him in the form of Bomber, who had arrived and was circling the crate, eyes widening with every pass he made.

'Beau,' Bomber yelled. 'Get down. GET DOWN NOW!'

Down? Beau thought. Was he kidding? He was so nearly there. He couldn't stop now. He wouldn't.

But Bomber was emphatic.

'Beau. I mean it. Get down and get down, now. Soldier, that IS AN ORDER!'

But there wasn't time, as a torrent of water flew in all directions, soaking not only Beau but Bomber too.

What followed was unexpected: a blur and whirl of fur and scales, and talons and teeth – lots of teeth.

It started with Mabel, screeching furiously from the water. She was soaked of course, drenched to her core, yet it didn't slow her down, and she tore over the lip of the crate, knocking an unsuspecting Beau off his climb and tumbling to the floor.

She landed flush on top of him, but didn't stop, her eyes wide with a panic that Beau had never seen before in animal or human. It was as though she had witnessed Hell at such close quarters it had blinded her, and she ricocheted around the carriage, bouncing off the walls and crate with every move she made.

'What's going on?' Beau cried.

'You don't want to know,' yelled Bomber, hovering soggily above the crate. 'Believe me, you DO NOT WANT TO KNOW!'

But then, as he backed away to the wall, Beau saw it. A long green jaw, breaking the water through the bars towards Bomber. There were teeth, long and white and sharp: they punctuated the gloom, snapping and snarling at the bird, who made sure he was nowhere in range.

'That's a . . . that's a . . . crocodile!' Beau howled. Three words that he never thought he would have to utter. But it was true, there was no denying it, and that was why Mabel looked so possessed, dashing from corner to corner, a trail of spray and unintelligible cries.

'Mabel,' Beau called, bounding after her unsuccessfully. 'Mabel, it's all right. You're safe now. You're safe. It can't get out, there are bars!'

But whatever he said, and no matter how many times he said it, she could not hear him. It was like she had the devil in her. She saw Beau, he swore she did, but it made no difference. She had been scared so deeply that she could not keep still, and in a last fit of fear and despair, she pinballed into the open doorway.

It all seemed to happen in slow motion. Mabel falling backwards, Beau screaming at her not to. Even Bomber's speed was no match for what was going on or what was about to occur.

Off-balance and terrified, Mabel tumbled through the door, the wintry wind pulling her soaking wet body, sucking it into its grasp.

'Nooooo!' cried Mabel. But it was too late. She tumbled from the carriage, and down to the tracks below, leaving Beau and Bomber totally powerless.

32

It was all too much.

First the Alfords, then the rats, then a crocodile . . . and now this?

'Can you see her?' Beau cried from the open doorway, as Bomber took flight. But the bird couldn't hear him, disappearing from sight as he flew in and out of the engine's smoke.

What should I do? Beau begged himself. *What should I do?*

He knew that he could do nothing. The train raced on, horn blaring, blissfully unaware of the drama at its rear. And at the very end of the tracks? Well, Peggy would be there, needing him, dreaming of him. If he wanted to get there quickly, then he had to stay onboard.

But now there was Mabel. And as much as he disliked her, and as much as he remembered how awful she was to him, the cat had saved him back on that first platform.

He looked for help, but there was none. Bomber had disappeared and his brain was simultaneously telling him to do two very different things.

He had to choose, and he had to choose quickly, so before he could stop his legs from moving, he shuffled forward into the open doorway.

It was terrifying, not knowing if he could safely jump clear, and he didn't know if he was brave enough to do it. But at the same time he was aware that every second he dallied could make the difference between saving Mabel or not. Every second took him further from her.

'I'm sorry, Peggy,' he whispered, before closing his eyes. 'I'm still coming, I really am.'

And with a final deep breath, he leaped into the wind, making his body as flat and aerodynamic as he possibly could.

He didn't see the earth coming to meet him. His eyes were screwed tightly closed, and in hindsight, that was probably a mistake, as it came as quite a shock when his body made impact. If he'd seen it hurtling towards him, he may have been able to make adjustments or brace himself. Instead, he bounced. He skidded. He rolled. He cried in pain and shock. The only positive Beau could possibly take from the fall was that the train missed him entirely, steaming past without pause or farewell. He'd also managed to clear the other tracks, and now lay on the grassy verge, not daring to move for fear of what his body would scream at him.

'Beau,' came a voice from above. It wasn't an angel welcoming him through the pearly gates; it was Bomber. 'That was one heck of a leap, soldier. Especially without a parachute.'

'Mabel,' Beau moaned. 'Did you find her? Is she all right?'

'Oh, I found her,' he replied. But he said little else, flying away so Beau had to follow him.

154

Every step hurt. But he limped on anyway, perturbed by his friend's silence about Mabel.

He saw them some two hundred yards down the track, though if Mabel was in pain, she was awfully good at hiding it. She was stalking from track to track, clearly talking nineteen to the dozen, though from his current range, Beau couldn't make out what was on her mind. He picked up the pace, or tried to, only slowing when he heard what was coming out of her mouth.

'I should have known,' she was raging, though whether it was to Bomber or herself wasn't clear. 'I mean, it's hardly breaking news is it, that dogs are trouble! Way more than they're worth. But I never thought for a million years that he'd lead me to a CROCODILE!'

Beau eyed her, incredulous, not just at what she was saying. 'Mabel . . .' he gaped. 'You're . . . all right?!'

'Oh, you think so, do you?' There was definitely nothing wrong with her lungs or mouth.

'Well, given that you just fell from a racing locomotive, I'd say you're in pretty rude health, yes.'

'Well, thank you, doctor,' she said resentfully. 'I'll be sure to come to you next time I'm savaged by a crocodile on your behalf.'

'*My* behalf?'

'Yes, yours. Of course, *yours*. I was on that train because of you, I was in that carriage because of you. I'm not at home, living the life of Riley . . . BECAUSE OF YOU. YOU, AND YOUR RIDICULOUS MISSION.'

Beau stood, aghast. It was hard to reply with his jaw dragging along the floor. But he gave it a darned good try.

'I didn't ask you to go into that carriage. I was going on my own before you raced ahead. I didn't ask you to get on the train either, or come with us to find Peggy. If you're here, it's because you've chosen to be, because maybe, deep down, you need to come as much as I do. You need to get to Wilf, just like me with Peggy.'

'That's ridiculous, nonsense, preposter—'

'And true,' cut in Beau. 'You know, there's nothing wrong in needing humans. Or even liking them for that matter.'

Mabel sneered her cattiest sneer. 'Cats don't need humans. Don't be so preposterous. All I need is mice on tap and a comfy bed.'

'That's crazy and you know it.'

'What's crazy,' argued Mabel, 'is that I was just savaged by a crocodile. I needed its affection as much as I need a human's.'

'It *was* a size too,' said Bomber, unhelpfully. 'I had the perfect vantage point from above. The water may have magnified it somewhat, but it was a big old beast.'

'It certainly felt that way,' Mabel replied, clearly relieved that the conversation had moved away from her motives for being there. 'Not that I was scared, of course.'

'No, that was clear from the way you ran around the carriage, howling like you were possessed,' Beau said.

'Well, at least I fought my way free. If it was you who'd fallen so bravely into that tank, then even *I* couldn't have saved you.'

'You know, you *could* just go home, Mabel?' Beau suggested. 'If Wilf really means so little to you?'

'Surely it would be quicker for me just to tag along till the end now.' Mabel shrugged, to accentuate how she really didn't give a hoot.

'Strength in numbers,' insisted Bomber. 'Especially in a world as crackpot as ours right now. I mean, London is on fire, the skies are full of bombs, and our trains are full of deadly reptiles.'

'Maybe,' said Mabel, 'we're *safer* on foot then. Not as many crocodiles to reckon with.'

'Safer, maybe,' added Beau, 'but an awful lot slower. Bomber, have you any idea where we are?'

'Of course,' the bird replied. 'Winchester is only an hour south-west for me. Four hours for you two.'

'Then we'll do it in three,' Beau said confidently. And despite his aching limbs and raging thirst, he set off behind Bomber, who, arrow-like, was pointing the way to Winchester.

33

They were not accosted by any savage or even vaguely aggressive animals between that point and Winchester. A cow or two turned their heads as they passed, one commenting that they 'weren't from round here', drawing a tut from its cud-munching partner, but that was all.

That wasn't the only positive. The search for water ended promptly too.

A quick, hard shower created puddles that all three of them lapped up, before they hit a stream, and whilst the water was icy cold, it was also blissful, Beau swearing blind that he could feel it easing the sting in every cut and bruise. It even gifted him back his sense of humour.

'Careful,' he shouted as Mabel leaned over the stream. 'I'm sure something in that stream just moved. You see that, Bomb?'

'Definitely,' replied the bird. 'Look, there it goes again!'

He saw Mabel yelp and dash back from the water's edge, pupils dilated in fear. Beau had no idea how long she'd remain on edge but pledged to enjoy every second of it. After all, she would if the roles were reversed.

Bomber brought them back to their mission, driving them on relentlessly, the pace never slowing, not even when the wind whipped and sang.

'Not far now,' he called on a number of occasions, his timing somehow serving as motivation instead of as an irritant, and when the spires of Winchester came into view, Beau wanted to bestow a medal on his rather brilliant chest.

'How many medals can a pigeon wear and still manage to fly?' Beau asked him.

'You'd be surprised,' came the reply. 'And we can test the theory as soon as we reach your Peggy.'

His friend's certainty pleased Beau. Winchester seemed pleasant enough, bustling, and although none of the children they passed in the streets could possibly be Peggy or Wilf, it made Beau long to find them even more.

'We have to do this, Bomber,' he whispered to his friend. 'We can't fail.'

'I don't even know what that word means,' Bomber replied. 'And I don't intend to learn.'

Dusk fell quickly, along with the temperature, and the streets quietened a little.

It was queer, unsettling. Beau had plenty of experience of being on the streets but it was the unfamiliarity of the area that made him feel on edge, and Bomber saw it.

'Dig in, soldier. Nothing to fear here. Shoulders back.'

Beau couldn't physically do that, but he *could* play to his strengths, which he did by pushing his nose to the floor, his senses coming alive as he detected the bounty on offer around him.

'That's tripe I can smell,' he whispered, almost romantically. 'You ever tried it, Bomb?'

'Can't say I have, no.'

'Not tempted?'

Bomber fixed him. 'You do know what tripe *is*, don't you?'

Beau didn't, not really. But he knew he liked it.

'What's your favourite meal then?'

That was easy. 'Seed.'

'Oh. Right.' It sounded dreadfully plain. 'Second favourite?'

'That'd be seed too.'

'And the third as well?'

Bomber nodded.

'You've never eaten anything except seed, have you?'

'Apart from those bits of batter you gave me, no. Why would I? Seed is fuel. It gives me everything I need to fulfil my duties. Job done.'

'Beats eating vermin, which is what certain other people round here would choose.' Beau tried to speak under his breath, but as usual Mabel was too sharp.

'In my eyes, dog, *you're* the verminous one, but I wouldn't entertain the thought of nibbling on you.' She side-eyed Bomber. 'Pigeons, on the other hand, are known as the rats of the sky . . . tasty.' She said nothing else. She didn't need to. It was enough to make Bomber fly that little bit further out of range, which meant Mabel went looking for her food in other directions, whilst Beau did the same, pushing his nose back to the tarmac.

It offered a rich variety of gastronomic delight. He smelled pastry and gravy from one house. Liver and onions from another. And if he wasn't mistaken, suet dumplings from a third. He craved them but didn't need them. He knew from experience that everything he needed to sustain him could be found in the bins behind these houses.

The food would be cold, and some of it on the turn, but as he tipped bins over, he found a veritable feast. It may have been slops, but to him, it was everything he'd dreamed of. He didn't care that Mabel returned to ridicule his lack of dining etiquette, he was simply doing what he needed to. Filling his belly so he could find his girl. Anything else was irrelevant.

Fifteen minutes later, the trio reconvened, bellies full, energy levels boosted.

'What have you eaten, Bomb?' asked Beau.

'Found a very hospitable dovecote round the corner. Smashing bunch. Very happy to share with a brave soldier like me.'

Mabel harrumphed, and said something unintelligible.

'So,' Beau said, 'what's the plan? Push on past Winchester and try to find a barn we can sleep in? Or find somewhere here? Stay here, and there's easy food on offer in the morning, I suppose.'

'A good point,' agreed Bomber. 'An army marches on its stomach.'

They looked to Mabel, fully expecting her to have a strong and vocal opinion of her own, but for once, she was silent. Silent and deathly still, her eyes fixed into the distance like she was witnessing her own death.

'Mabel?' Beau said, once then twice, nudging her with his nose when he got no response. 'Mabel!'

But when she remained lost in her thoughts, Beau followed her gaze, and saw what had stolen her attention.

There, on the high street, lit by flaming torches, stood the most outrageously dressed and beautiful woman Beau had ever locked eyes on. She was dressed in a long, flowing gown made from animal skin, with a slit from the ankle to the very top of her left thigh. Her skin seemed to shine, but not as brightly as the bangles that lined each of her wrists. Beau drank her in, her hair sitting proudly in a vast, rich cloud, a single pink flower tucked neatly above her right ear, and a pair of extravagant hooped earrings. She was beautiful, divine and feminine, but at the same time, she was steely. Her cheeks were powdered with rouge and her lashes stretched longer than seemed humanly possible, but it was her eyes that burned brightest. It may have been a trick of the fading light, but they seemed to be flame-orange, and Beau feared that if he looked too long at her, he may fall under her spell, just as Mabel clearly had.

However, it was then, and only then, that Beau realised what had really entranced and terrified his compatriot, as from behind the woman's gown prowled an animal on a lead, the chain stretched tautly as the beast strained against it.

But this was no dog being walked. As hard as it was to believe, the animal on the lead was a crocodile, the same one that had so nearly cost Mabel her life only hours earlier.

34

The animals weren't the only ones who couldn't believe their eyes.

From every corner of the street, people moved cautiously forward to a chorus of gasps and stage whispers.

'*It's not,*' they whispered. '*It can't be!*'

'It flipping well is,' mouthed Mabel, the first sign of life from her in a good minute or so. Unlike the others, she showed no interest whatsoever in moving any closer.

'Tonight!' bellowed a man from behind the striking and beautiful woman. 'For one night only, here at the Theatre Royal Winchester! Witness the unwitnessable, believe the unbelievable, step inside the mesmeric world of the one and only Koringa . . . and her faithful crocodile, Churchill!'

There was a titter from the crowd. The reptile may have been as pugnacious as the prime minister, but there were no other physical similarities that anyone could see.

'What do you think she does with the crocodile?' Beau wondered, open-mouthed.

'I don't know. And I don't want to know either,' Mabel replied.

She was alone in that thought, however. Beau, and Bomber in particular, were captivated by the sight in front of them.

'That woman,' the bird said, 'is a goddess. A true warrior goddess. Look at her. She could take down Hitler single-handedly, with or without the crocodile.'

'Tickets ARE still available,' bleated the man, again and again. 'See her walk barefoot on broken glass. See her submerged in a pit of live serpents. See her put her head in Churchill's mouth!'

If ever there was a statement that would draw gasps, that was it, followed by a thunderclap of footsteps as people of all ages swarmed towards the box office.

Beau looked at Bomber. Bomber looked at Beau. Mabel still stared at Churchill.

'I think we should stay in town tonight,' added Bomber. 'After all, it looks like rain.'

'I am *not* going anywhere near that theatre,' said Mabel. 'And besides, since when did they start offering free tickets to animals? Or ANY tickets, for that matter?'

'Oh, we'll get in, don't you worry,' smiled Bomber.

'In the stalls? Or will you book the royal box?'

'Oh, I don't think we'll be mixing with the hoi polloi. But I'll get us in. I'm a spy, you know, as well as a soldier.'

'Of course you are,' Mabel sighed, which only made Beau laugh.

'Spy away then,' he said, and watched with glee as Bomber tore off in search of the best seats in the house.

The next few minutes comprised of Mabel pacing nervously in the shadows, and Beau, for once, forgetting about

Peggy. Was it true, what the man had said? Would this Koringa do what he said she would? Because unless the crocodile was suddenly sedated, he couldn't believe it would end in anything but a massacre.

Before long, Bomber returned, swooping down with purpose and poise.

'Easy,' he said. 'Follow me.' Beau duly did, although Mabel took a lot more persuading.

Eventually, they found themselves at the stage door at the rear of the building.

'Stay here. Wait for the distraction, then dash in. I'll meet you at the top of the second flight of stairs.'

'Distraction? What distraction?' hissed Mabel, still looking for an escape, but Bomber had already sped off like a bullet, heading straight for a burly man who stood guard by the open door.

The next few moments were a blur of feathers and beak and foul language, though only the first two came from Bomber, as he thrust himself at the man's face, circling him, pecking at his ears and neck. The man was shocked. How could he be anything else? In his surprise and panic, he stumbled away from the doorway, batting at the unperturbed bird.

'That looks like a distraction to me!' barked Beau and he dashed forward, pushing Mabel along with him as they tore, unnoticed, through the door and up the dingy staircase in front of them.

'I thought theatres were glamorous places,' moaned Mabel.

'Does it matter?' replied Beau, tearing up the second flight as instructed. 'Just do as you're told, for once in your life.'

She did, reluctantly, grumbling with every step, but by the time they reached the top of the next flight, Bomber was already waiting for them.

'How did you get there?' Mabel seemed affronted at his stealth.

'Wings and an open window, what more does a bird need?' And he led them on up two more flights of threadbare stairs.

'Surely that's high enough,' Mabel gasped, as Bomber told Beau to press hard against a peeling, wooden door.

The sight on the other side made the climb worthwhile however.

They were not in the auditorium, not as such, but perched high to the side of the stage. They could see out to the right row upon row of plush red velvet seats, filling fast with wide-eyed children and excited adults.

In front of the animals ran several metal bars, holding drapes and lights, and there, deep below, was the wooden stage floor with footlights winking its entire length.

'That glamorous enough for you?' whispered Beau to Mabel, and she could not deny it. There was something magical about this place. A reverence, a history and an unquestionable buzz of anticipation. This was a place where special things happened, and none of them could wait to witness what those might be.

They didn't have long to wait, as suddenly the lights went

down, plunging the world into darkness. A buzz of excitement rippled through the crowd, followed by a slow swell of exotic, mesmerising music, played by a small band in the orchestra pit. The notes ebbed and flowed, rose and fell, and Beau felt entranced by them, a feeling which only increased when a single spotlight hit the stage to reveal Koringa in all her beauty.

Gone was the ballgown, replaced now by a sequined leopard print swimsuit, but she looked no less breathtaking. She was a queen, her magnificent hair sitting proudly like a crown on her head. There was a gasp from the audience, followed by applause, despite the fact that she hadn't yet moved. She seemed almost affronted by this, silencing the crowd with a sharp whip of her arm.

From the shadows strode four other women, all of them beautiful, but there was no doubt that they were apprentices to the sorceress. They moved like silk around her, waving their arms in front of her face, until slowly, Koringa started to sway. The rhythm built, her movements following suit, eventually becoming so dramatic it was a wonder she could stay on her feet.

'What is going on?' Beau whispered.

'SHHHH!' replied the other two. They hadn't a clue, but they didn't want to miss a beat.

And rightly so, as suddenly Koringa fell backwards, her body completely rigid, only to be caught by one of her minions, who made an almighty show of just how hypnotised and heavy her mistress was.

Slowly and dramatically they lifted her up, one assistant at her shoulders and another at her feet, as if she were on an imaginary stretcher, before placing her so her neck and ankles rested across the seats of two wooden chairs. The rest of her body didn't move.

'This is bizarre!' said Beau.

'But brilliant,' added Bomber, who hadn't blinked since the lights went down.

'Look! LOOK!' added Mabel, nodding towards the four assistants, who were carrying a *huge* slab of concrete onto the stage, before balancing it on the abdomen of Koringa. She did not even flinch.

Beau had questions, but he didn't have time to ask them as the drama continued. Now the jeopardy was raised another notch with the arrival of a sledgehammer, so big and heavy that it looked like it belonged in the muscular arms of a god.

The show was really about to begin.

35

'Er, am I ill and seeing things, or is this really happening?'

Bomber stared onwards, 'It's real. But if that hammer is here for the reason I'm imagining, it's Koringa who is about to get very, very poorly.'

The animals watched in horror as one of the assistants climbed upon a third chair, hoisting the heavy hammer high above her head.

There were screams from the audience, cries of 'Stop!' and 'Don't do it!' but they fell on deaf ears as the hammer came thudding down, landing on the concrete slab with a sickening thud.

The room gasped as one. But the stone did not break and Koringa did not move.

It happened a second time, then a third and a fourth, the gasps growing louder and more frenzied. It was only when the hammer fell for a fifth time that the slab gave up and split in two, falling to the floor in a cloud of dust and delirious cheers which only got louder as the smoke cleared to reveal Koringa still in her horizontal trance, unmoved and unhurt.

'HOW DID SHE DO THAT?' Beau yelped amongst the applause.

'It can't be real,' sneered Mabel.

'What the hammer? Or the concrete? Did you not hear the noise it made?'

'A sound effect. A drum or something.'

Fortunately, the action came so thick and fast that it kept any bickering at bay.

Koringa's bravery, if not lunacy, seemed to know no bounds. As the man outside had promised, she *did* walk barefoot across broken glass, she *did* escape from a pit filled with angry snakes, she even climbed and danced on a ladder whose rungs were made of sharpened sword blades. It was, without doubt, like nothing the three of them had ever seen.

But then it was time for the main event. The pinnacle. The arrival of Churchill onstage, and he appeared with venom, still attached to his lead and dragging not one but two assistants with him. Mabel pushed herself backwards, deeper into the shadows. Churchill snapped and lurched at his handlers, even in the direction of the audience, which drew a series of pantomime boos and hisses.

His rowdy misbehaviour didn't last long though, because Koringa strode over, and in one decisive movement, swept down and plucked the crocodile skywards, tucking him under her arm, not flinching or panicking when Churchill sought to remove her fingers.

It was the craziest of spectacles. A fight no human should have won, but within twenty seconds, Koringa had deposited the animal on a table, walking slowly to its head, ignoring its wildly snapping jaws as she waved her hands in front of it.

The crowd bellowed and squealed. Beau saw one man fanning his child with his hat, such was their queasiness, but there was no need to worry. As Koringa's hands waved and beckoned, Churchill's snapping became less frequent, and his head began to sag. Before long his jaw hung limply open, eyes fixed dozily on his mistress, who continued to entrance him.

'That crocodile . . . is hypnotised!' stammered Beau.

'Don't be ridiculous,' came Mabel's reply. 'It must be drunk.'

'Do you see a whisky bottle anywhere? I'm telling you, that woman is a WITCH!'

'I think the word you're looking for,' added Bomber, 'is a fakir.'

'A fa-what?'

'Fakir. People who are specialists in magic or sorcery. OH MY GOODNESS, WHAT IS SHE DOING NOW?'

He was right to ask, as two of Koringa's assistants had positioned themselves either side of Churchill, and in his weakened state, had levered his jaws open as wide as they could possibly go. Then they let go, dramatically backing away to allow their mistress to advance, lowering her head until all of it sat within the crocodile's jaws.

There she stayed for ten, twenty, thirty seconds. The crocodile did not move and nor did Koringa. The assistants began to agitate Churchill, to poke him with sticks, but it made no difference. The fakir remained firmly at the beast's mercy until finally, with a flourish, she removed herself from his jaws, and with a single clap, released Churchill from his trance too. The result was instantaneous. Gone was the sedated, obedient animal, to be replaced once more by a snapping, hungry beast.

With a forward leap, the four assistants tethered the crocodile, and with a huge amount of struggle, ushered him from the stage, leaving Koringa to take her bow.

The applause. Was. Deafening.

People were on their feet, and the adulation washed over Koringa, bouncing off the stage walls and rolling to the heavens where the three animals sat.

They said nothing and did nothing. They could not believe what they had witnessed, nor explain it, and they stayed that way, even when the curtain fell, the house lights came up and the audience filed reluctantly out.

'What do we do now?' asked Mabel.

'We wait till it's empty,' replied Bomber. 'Otherwise I don't fancy our chances of you two escaping unseen.'

This seemed fair enough, and the trio sat contemplatively, until every living soul had disappeared from view and the lights had been extinguished. They looked at each other and heard one final door slam some floors below them.

Then, and only then did they start to descend the stairs.

'Same plan applies on the way out, just in case there's a straggler lying in wait,' stated Bomber matter-of-factly. 'If there is, look for the distraction, then straight out the stage door.'

But as Bomber flew through the open window it seemed no distraction was needed, as there wasn't a soul in sight.

'Do you really think everyone's gone?' asked Beau.

'Looks that way.'

Beau stopped on the final dark stair, the stage door smack bang in front of them. But just to its right was a large glass tank with bars on the top.

'Is that Churchill's?' Beau asked, straining into the darkness.

'Looks like it,' Mabel gulped.

'And can you see him in there?'

'Not yet,' Mabel said, squinting into the gloom.

'Right ... well. After you,' said Beau, waving the cat through.

'Oh, no, no, no. After you.'

Beau took a deep breath and moved forward.

36

They should've dashed past the tank and out of the door for a number of reasons.

They had a mission to fulfil for a start, and an expectant bird waiting outside. And there was the small matter of being utterly terrified of the crocodile lurking inside the tank.

But as they sneaked up to it, they were stopped unexpectedly.

'It's you, isn't it?' a voice called to them, which scared them half to death as they had no idea where it was coming from.

Beau scrabbled against the stage door but it wouldn't give. Mabel did the same.

'I know it's you,' came the voice again. 'I can *smell* you. People don't realise how good our sense of smell is. But I'd recognise you anywhere. You almost came for lunch earlier, didn't you? On the train?'

Both animals gulped, their stomachs lurching.

'I know it's you. You smell . . . tasty.'

For once in her life, Mabel was speechless, and she threw herself against the door once more in the vain hope that it would magically open for her.

Her actions drew laughter, not from Beau, but from Churchill.

'Come on now, calm yourself down. I'm only pulling your leg, which does, incidentally, look tasty.'

This did little to calm Mabel down.

'I'm sorry, I'm sorry,' Churchill went on. 'That was uncalled for. It's just I recognised your scent, but I couldn't work out for the life of me why you'd come back after what happened earlier.'

'Ask this fool,' hissed Mabel, looking at Beau.

'It wasn't just me,' Beau said, 'it was Bomber too.' Before he remembered the bird wasn't there to back him up. 'We heard what the man said about your act out on the street. It was hard to walk on after that.'

'Yes,' the crocodile sighed. 'He is quite the salesman. And a taskmaster to boot.'

'It was just about the most incredible thing I've ever seen in my life,' Beau went on, approaching the tank and peering at the creature inside.

'Can we just leave?' Mabel hissed. 'I hardly think he needs your compliments given the whole theatre was on their feet for him.'

'So? It doesn't hurt to be polite, you know. I must ask, though. How does she do it?'

'Who?'

'Koringa. How does she hypnotise you like she does?'

'Oh that,' he grinned, a row of pearly teeth gleaming like keys on a grand piano. 'A magician never reveals her secrets. And neither does her crocodile.'

'But the change in you from when you first came on stage – you were so angry. Furious! You have to tell us!'

'Beau! *Come on!*' hissed Mabel.

'I'm delighted you enjoyed my performance,' Churchill replied, oblivious. 'I've been working on it for some time. Years, in fact.'

'Years?' Beau said. 'You must have been *everywhere* in that time.'

'Twice,' Churchill nodded proudly. 'Though I must admit, I don't see quite as much of "everywhere" as my mistress. Just train carriages, the occasional street to sell some tickets, backstages . . .' He sounded unimpressed. '. . . and the faces of the crowds when I scare them to death. That's the moment I live for.'

Beau was surprised. Not at the last bit, but at the monotony of the rest of it.

'And what is she like? Koringa?'

'She's my mistress.'

'Yes, I know, but what's she *like*?'

'*Like?*'

'Yes. My mistress Peggy's funny and kind. And she treats me better than anyone else ever could. Feeds me scraps under the table. Even if she knows full well she's going to get caught. Your Koringa, does she give you treats?'

'Her people feed me. When I'm hungry. When I need it to perform.'

Beau was surprised. His attitude to food sounded like Bomber's, which seemed dreadfully dull.

'But she must love having you. I mean, the act you put on out there. It was amazing.'

Churchill looked perplexed. 'We have a relationship based on mutual respect and necessity.'

Beau had no idea what that meant. Not really.

'Sorry?'

'I do what's necessary. My job. She entertains. I entertain. We pack up. We move on and we do it again. Seven nights a week, twice on Wednesdays and Fridays. Christmas Day and Easter Sunday? We rest.'

Beau scowled. All of a sudden it didn't sound quite so glamorous. He looked at the tank, and for the first time saw it as something different. It wasn't a tank, it was a cage. Yes, the sides might be glass, but the bars on top still trapped Churchill inside. Without a choice. With no way of escape.

'Don't you ever want something different?' Beau asked.

'Like what?'

'I don't know, to be outside, on the street, anywhere without your lead? To have a human praise you, or feed you out of pleasure instead of duty? Don't you want to be . . . free?'

Beau heard Mabel splutter behind him. 'It really is time we went,' she said, urgently.

'In a minute,' Beau replied, before turning back to Churchill. 'What if I were to unlock those bars for you before we leave?'

'What good would that do?' came the reply.

'He's right,' said Mabel quickly. 'So let's go.'

But Beau wasn't having it. 'What do you mean, what good would it do? We'd be giving you a choice. A chance to be free. On your own terms.'

Churchill sighed. 'And where would I go exactly? From the little I've seen there are no swamps round here for me to slide into. And even if there were, how would I get there without causing panic? Without being shot? What would you have me do, squeeze down the lavatory and live in the sewers? And even if I did, can you really tell me that I'd live a better life that way? There won't be fresh meat to eat. Or adoring crowds either.'

He wasn't angry, just resigned. And that added to the sense of sadness that Beau felt. Because even though Beau was heading towards a very sad little girl, at least when he got there, he would have the freedom to support her, to walk alongside her, to feel whatever she was feeling. He would have choices. And Churchill wouldn't.

So, without saying another word, he found an old wooden chair and pushed it with his nose to the edge of the tank.

'Beau!' spat Mabel, terrified now. 'What are you doing? Stop it now.'

But he didn't listen. Instead, he clambered onto the chair and onto his hind legs, his nose now at the top of the tank, just inches from Churchill's. Furiously, Mabel leaped up and knocked him to the floor. She didn't stop there either, pushing Beau onto his back and pinning him with unexpected strength.

'Beau!' she hissed. 'What's come over you?'

'What do you mean?'

'*What do I mean?* There's a wild animal in that tank. A killer. I know, because it tried to eat me earlier!'

Beau struggled against her.

'Don't be so ridiculous, dog! Where are we going now, Beau? Where are we heading to?'

'To Peggy, you know that.'

'That's right. And why?'

'Because she needs us.'

'Why else?'

'Because she'll be sad.'

'Why else?'

'Well . . . to keep her safe, of course.'

'That's right!' Mabel spat. 'Because she's a little girl that you love, and more than anything you want her to be safe. Correct?'

'Of course!' This all seemed obvious to Beau.

'But at the same time, you want to set a dangerous animal free. A crocodile who has never had that luxury in its life.' Mabel lowered her voice before she went on, 'Now, I'm not saying that he's evil, but he's never been free around people before! How would you feel if he went and hurt someone, even by accident? How would you feel if he killed a child?'

Her final words hit him like a slap, and his limbs went limp. He didn't know what to say.

'Because if it were Wilf he hurt, or Peggy, for that matter, I'd never forgive *myself*. Never mind *you*.'

And there Beau had it. Mabel was right. He couldn't remember a previous time in his life when he'd agreed with her so readily, or when she had quite simply been so . . . right.

What had he been thinking, even *considering* setting the crocodile free?

'I'm sorry,' he said. 'It was silly of me. More than silly. I don't know what came over me.'

'Yes, well, it's not like I don't expect it from you, is it?'

Beau felt shame burn deep in him as Mabel let him go. But he also noticed she seemed a little sheepish herself, and as he thought about why that might be, he realised she'd given away far more of herself than she could possibly have meant to. She'd admitted very clearly that she not only cared for Wilf, but for Peggy too.

He stretched his aching limbs, and as he did so, he thought about telling Mabel what he'd heard in her words. Then he remembered how sharp her claws had felt when she'd pinned him down. Perhaps it was enough for him to know she had a heart, even if she kept it stashed deep inside her.

Maybe, he thought, as Mabel leaped effortlessly at the door handle, this realisation might make the next part of their journey just that little bit easier.

37

Within minutes, Beau wondered if he was wrong. Mabel clearly didn't have a heart after all.

'I don't know what you thought you were doing back there,' she said, head shaking judgementally, 'but it was the most irresponsible thing I have ever witnessed in my life.'

'Look, I know I got carried away. And I know it was daft. And reckless. But I couldn't stop thinking about how all Churchill ever sees is that tank and a stage every day. It can't be pleasant never knowing where you really are one day to the next, never having someone around who truly cares or loves you?'

'He's a WILD ANIMAL, you fool, not a guinea pig.'

'Doesn't mean he doesn't have feelings. And you heard him, his life is repetitive and not of his choosing.'

'He has hundreds of people on their feet every day, either running from him or cheering him from the rafters. Now, I don't know about you, dog, but that's the kind of adulation I wouldn't mind. So you shouldn't have even *thought* about setting him free.'

Beau let his thoughts gather. He didn't need reminding (again) that he had been in the wrong, but at the same time, he had seen something that was missing in Churchill's life but which Beau had in abundance (whenever Peggy was around at least). Beau had a person who lived *for* him, lived *with* him: someone who wanted to share whatever they had. And he knew that a life without that didn't seem like a life worth having.

They trotted on. Beau was in pain. He felt it in his belly, around his neck and on his rump. He was starting to flag.

Fortunately, he had Bomber, who like the true commanding officer he was, saw Beau needed his help.

'The hours of darkness are always the worst,' he said from above. 'And you know what follows night, don't you?'

'Eight hours' sleep, if you're a cat worth their salt,' answered Mabel. 'Eight hours with a blissfully full stomach.'

'Speak when you're spoken to,' said Bomber curtly. 'Dawn, Beau. Dawn comes next, and with that comes a whole new day, with new challenges, but new opportunities too. And when dawn comes, you'll be closer to Peggy by some distance.'

Beau liked the sound of that. 'How far is it now, Bomb? To the coast, I mean?'

'Hard to say. Thirty-five miles? Possibly more.'

It sounded like a lot.

'But if we keep going now, if you keep following the path that your officer shows you, I promise I'll get you there in the shortest time possible. Do you hear me? You have my word, as a soldier.'

'And a pigeon,' added Mabel, sarcastically.

They ignored her and carried on, despite the darkness.

It didn't so much affect Beau or Mabel. The former still had his nose to rely on, and Mabel was very used to hunting at night. It was just more challenging for Bomber. He'd never flown this route in the dark, and it made it harder for him to spot landmarks that would keep them on track. There were occasional wrong turns that walked them into barbed wire, painful undergrowth and hidden bogs, which Mabel moaned about obviously. But they didn't stop. They kept going, pausing only to lap at the occasional puddle, or if they were lucky, a stream. They should have slept. Too many hours had passed since Beau's nap on the train, but he daren't think about stopping. Rest for too long, and he wasn't sure if he'd get back up again.

'Did you always know war was coming?' Beau asked Bomber, shortly before dawn. They hadn't spoken for a while, and Beau could feel his legs stiffening. He hoped a conversation might take his mind off it but knew better than to seek one from the cat skulking beside them.

'I think I did,' Bomber replied, having given it due thought and consideration. 'It was a word I remember from when I was very young. The man who fed us, he talked about it all the time. Things he'd heard on the wireless, the maps in the newspaper, showing where Hitler was marching. And the old birds would tell us stories from the last war. Ones that had been passed down from generation to generation, egg to egg. Things the birds had done.'

'Like what?'

'Imagine this,' Bomber began. 'Mile upon mile of battered fields. Craters like those on the moon. Tailfins of bombs dug into the earth, some exploded, others waiting to be trodden on.'

'Gosh, this is a happy story when morale is already so high, isn't it?' moaned Mabel.

'Imagine barbed wire that coils on for miles, protecting trenches where thousands of men huddle knee-deep in putrid water. Those men would wait days, weeks, sometimes months to advance even fifteen feet. Some men were brave, sent into no-man's-land to survey the opposition's trenches. And if they managed to return in once piece, they had to communicate this to the officers, who were often miles behind the front line.'

'Which is where you came in?'

'Exactly. They'd hide messages, or maps, or an SOS in canisters strapped to birds' legs. They might be of the utmost importance, the sort of intelligence that could win a battle, affect a whole war. And they trusted us to deliver it.'

'I can see the headline now – *Bird flies*. How exciting,' Mabel sighed.

'That's just it though, cat, it *was* exciting. And thrilling. And dangerous. You see, the Germans, they knew what we were doing. And they'd shoot at the pigeons every second they were in the air. Round upon round – but these birds, they were brave. One bird flew over fifty missions, another lost an eye and a foot but still delivered its message. One bird flew twenty miles in twenty minutes, saving a dozen lives as it did it so.

They were heroes. Every last one of them. And once I heard about them, how could I possibly want to be anything else?'

It made sense, to Beau at least. And it made him even fonder of Bomber, as well as steeling himself.

'So if you could do one thing, Bomber, during the war, what would that be?'

The bird looked at him. 'I'm doing it, aren't I? I'm getting you to Peggy.'

'Yes, but after? Because we're going to achieve that, aren't we?'

Bomber thought about this as he flew. 'We are, of course we are. But when the call comes, all I know is that it will come from the air. I want to do what no other war pigeon has done. To fly alongside one of our own – a Spitfire, or a Hurricane, as they tear towards the Luftwaffe. I may only be a bird, I'm not daft, but I can do my bit, just like the old birds did. And I will. I can feel it.'

It was a sentiment that was hard to disagree with, and it fuelled not only Beau's imagination, filling his brain with images of bird and machine in perfect fighting symmetry, but his limbs with a much-needed energy too. On he went, stride after stride, yard after yard, mile after mile, until without noticing, dawn broke around them. They were edging closer. He could smell it.

38

It was a sight Beau had neither seen nor imagined.

Fields, rolling left to right, kissing the horizon as far as he could see. There wasn't a car, a cart, or a person in view, even dwellings were scarce and hard to pick out. The distant smoke from early-morning fires were the only sign of life.

October had dampened the colours of the fields, whilst threads of low-lying mist clung to the ground in others, giving an atmosphere that Beau had never experienced before. Fog in London often felt mysterious, threatening even. But here it felt magical, and as they sat for a long-awaited rest, Beau felt his pulse drop and his limbs relax as the clouds drifted away in places, revealing more fields, more birds, a more people-less life.

'That, my friends, was an excellent night's progress,' Bomber declared. Beau nodded encouragingly.

Mabel looked less impressed. At Bomber's declaration anyway. But she seemed very impressed with the shrew that she was currently devouring.

'I don't need another motivational speech from you,' she declared. 'I've heard so many, they're starting to lose their impact. Just tell me how many more hours I have to trudge across these godforsaken fields.'

'You do know you don't have to come with us, don't you,

Mabel?' interrupted Beau. 'And before you say it's just to keep me out of trouble, let me say this: I don't believe you. That's not the reason and you know it.'

'You really are tiresome, hound. I don't know what you're talking about.'

'Oh, I think you do. You talk, all the time, on and on about how you don't need anybody. But I've seen you, and I know different.'

'Do you now?'

'Yes, I do. You think I didn't see you every morning, slipping into Wilf's bed when he got up for school?'

'Why waste a comforting warm spot?'

'That's not why. You got in to feel close to him. Even if he wasn't there.'

'Preposterous,' Mabel replied, but she seemed unusually ruffled.

'Is it? Then why did you do the same after he'd gone? Why get into his bed when he wasn't even there to warm it up first?'

Mabel did not like this. But for once she chose not to argue further with Beau, and instead turned her back on him, directing her words only to Bomber.

'How long till Bournemouth?'

'Three hours, four at most,' Bomber replied.

'Then let's go,' she said, matter of factly, before walking on.

Beau looked at Bomber, who shrugged.

Why couldn't she just admit she had feelings for anyone other than herself? Beau thought, as he pulled himself to his aching feet.

He wasn't sure which hurt most, the tender pads on his paws, or the cuts and bruises everywhere else. But he knew his pain would be nothing compared to what Peggy would be feeling. *His* pain would keep him alert, would drive him on, so hers could ultimately be eased.

They set off again, their paws smudging the early morning dew, the only noise the sound of their breathing as they climbed another and another of the rolling hills. They found a rhythm that lasted a good two or more hours. It felt peaceful, and for once, safe. Like there was nothing that could throw them off balance or knock them from their path.

But as the world started to wake, something new could be heard. Softly at first, then louder, and louder.

It sounded like a musical instrument. A horn, perhaps. But what became apparent very quickly was that either the instrument, or its player, possessed only a very limited range.

'What on earth is that?' Beau asked.

'Bit early for a recital,' added Bomber as he took to the sky.

'Both the tune and the musician are terrible,' said Mabel.

But it continued regardless, the animals' confusion increasing as they tried unsuccessfully to work out where it was coming from. It seemed to bounce from every hillside and was very unsettling. Not as unsettling as being knocked unceremoniously off your feet, which is exactly what happened to Mabel, as two bundles of fur suddenly whipped past, upending themselves too in the process.

The first one barked a torrent of words turning the air

blue before he had even finished tumbling; the second exclaimed her displeasure using words that none of them understood.

It wasn't until they finally came to a standstill, their fur bristling, that Beau could see what they were dealing with: foxes.

One of them (he of the foul tongue) was clearly a male and despite living in such pastoral surroundings, he had a streetwise quality to him that Beau recognised. His movements were quick and jerky, and he had a habit of constantly looking behind and around him, as if he were being chased. His face was long and lean, and etched with scars old and new, whilst his muzzle sniffed continually, presumably weighing up the danger that these new visitors presented.

The second fox was everything the first one wasn't. She was beautiful, for a start. A deep, autumnal red which seemed to set the air around her ablaze. There was a stillness to her, but also a distrust. She continually held her head cocked to one side, and she took up a position behind the male, as if using him as a shield.

'Watch where you're going, will you?' the male spat at them, his voice thick with anger.

'I think you'll find we were standing still . . .' Mabel was not intimidated. 'And besides, what's the rush? Not exactly much going on round here.'

The male snarled in reply. 'What do you want then?' he said, before noticing Beau, who was doing his friendliest tail wag, as if to make up for Mabel's lack of manners.

It didn't help though. If anything it made things worse. The female cowered instantly, shaking, pushing herself closer to her protector, which only served to make the male growl and tense its limbs, seemingly ready to pounce.

'What you after?' he growled at Beau. 'We don't like your type.'

'Well, I'm glad it's not just me,' sighed Mabel. 'Perhaps we can be friends after all. I'm Mabel. And you are?'

'I'm furious.'

'Furious?' Mabel couldn't help but laugh.

'Furious you'd have the cheek to come on our land with a hound, when you clearly know what that would do to our nerves. Especially my love's.'

Mabel looked bemused. 'I don't know what you mean.'

The male sneered. 'Oh, I think you do. I think you know what happens when a fox meets a hound.'

'. . . er . . .'

'Where you been living? On the moon?'

'No, London.'

'Don't they have fox hunting there?'

'Not so I've seen. Though if I found a fox hunting on my patch, I can't say I'd be too happy about it.'

Beau had been listening and trying to take it in, but most of all he'd been watching the fretful face of the female, still cowering behind her mate.

'Listen, I'm sorry if me being here is a problem,' he offered. 'The last thing we want to do is scare you . . .'

'A likely story,' growled the fox.

'It's true. All we're doing, the three of us, is passing through. On the way to the coast. To find my girl. You see, her parents were killed in a bomb.'

It was a lot to take in, and the fox looked even more confused when the dog and cat were joined by a proud-chested pigeon, who landed on Beau's back.

'It's true,' Bomber remarked. 'Everything he said. I know about fox hunts, though. I know what they do to innocents like you, but I also know my friend here, who is the most kind-hearted of soldiers.'

'Soldiers?' The male didn't like the sound of that.

And Bomber realised his mistake. 'A true soldier doesn't go looking for trouble. Not like the beasts that hunt *you* down. Real soldiers will do anything to avoid death or violence. You must believe me.'

'I don't have to believe anything you say,' the fox replied. 'You heard the horn, didn't you? You know what that means. It means they're coming.'

Beau suddenly made the connection between the horn and its meaning.

'But it's miles away, that noise.'

'It is for now. But do you know how fast their horses are? Do you know how fit them dogs are? Lungs like locomotives and teeth like razors. That combination is not good for anyone, let me tell you.'

As if on cue, there was another call from the horn. Still

192

distant, but closer, and it brought a frantic response from the female. She started to prowl and pace behind her partner, before pushing her muzzle against his, murmuring something fretful into his fur.

'Is she all right?' Beau asked.

'Does she look it?'

'Well, no, but I couldn't understand what she was saying.'

'Well, you wouldn't. And neither do I. Cos she's French.'

'French?' The three friends looked to each other. This was another unexpected twist, and they turned to the male, waiting for him to fill in the gaps.

39

'Yes. French. As in France. The place. The country.'

'We're aware of it,' said Mabel, coolly.

'Right. Well, I think she's French, anyway. I'm not totally sure.'

It didn't make much sense to Beau.

'But what's a fox from France doing here?'

'Isn't it obvious?' he snapped.

'Well, no. Not to me.'

'She's *here* because of *your* sort. Your sort and their so-called sport.' He looked angry, but also emotional. 'Used to be packed with foxes, these fields. Hundreds of us. And we weren't bothering no one. Well, 'cept chickens, maybe. But according to the humans, we was vermin. According to them, we was dangerous. So the horses came, with the people on 'em. All dressed in those red coats. And they brought their hounds, so many of them that we didn't stand a chance.' He paused and nuzzled his partner, who looked no less distressed. He lowered his voice a little as he went on, 'They came and they came and they came, hunting and hunting, month after month. And they did it for so long, that in the end there were hardly any of us left.'

'I'm so sorry,' Beau sighed. 'But if that's the case, why are they still hunting, if there's no danger left?'

'There was no danger in the first place! We're just living here, like the other animals, aren't we? All right, we might be less useful. We might not give 'em eggs or milk or cheese. No, they weren't hunting us cos of danger.'

'Then why were they doing it?'

'Because they love it. The hunt, the thrill, the chase. They call it sport, don't they? And when there were hardly any of us left, they still weren't prepared to stop. They called meetings. Came up with a plan to go overseas. To Germany, Italy, France. They paid people to hunt *foreign* foxes down, but not kill 'em. Just catch 'em, sail 'em 'ere and set 'em free. Do that enough times, get the new foxes breeding, and then the sport don't ever have to stop, does it?'

Beau didn't know what to say. It sounded ridiculous, far-fetched, but from the look on the two foxes' faces, he feared it had to be true.

'I'm . . . I'm sorry,' he said softly. 'That's . . . awful. So your partner here, they sailed her from France?'

'After they kidnapped her, yeah, I reckon so. She just turned up in my den, didn't she? Out of nowhere. Covered in cuts and the stink of hounds. She'd got away from 'em. Lord knows how, but she managed it. In a right state, she was. Fever for days. She was saying all this stuff, but I hadn't a clue what it meant. All I knew was that she was the most beautiful thing I'd ever laid eyes on. I had to make her well again.'

'Well, it looks like you did,' Beau said.

'What's her name?' asked Bomber.

'Not exactly sure. There was one word she kept saying in the early days. *Renard*, she'd repeat. *Renard. Renard.* So that's who she is. Renard.' He turned to her, expression softening, tongue licking a blade of grass from her cheek. 'It's all right, Renard. I'm here. I'll keep you safe.'

It was clear to Beau that this fox was doing his best to put her at ease, despite not knowing what she was saying. And that was love, pure and simple.

'Where you going again? Coast, was it?' the male fox asked, making a point of aiming the question at Mabel and Bomber.

'That's right,' said Mabel.

'Anvil Point lighthouse,' said Beau.

'Never heard of it. Never heard of a human being worth that kind of effort neither. Monsters. All of 'em.'

'Not Peggy. She's different. She's special.'

'Course she is,' said the fox dryly. 'But you *would* say that. You're a hound. She's probably got 'er own horse already. Just a matter of time till she's after the likes of us.'

'No,' Beau said firmly. 'Peggy's not like that. And never will be. She saved me. Took me in. Gave me love when no one else would.' He took a step towards the foxes and saw them flinch in return. Especially the vixen. 'I know you won't believe this. But I'm like you. *Just* like you. Humans have treated me badly in the past. Sticks, boots, belts. There wasn't anything they wouldn't hit me with. They didn't feed me. Didn't brush my coat or stroke me. Made me sleep outside with no shelter, regardless of the weather. So when they dumped me in an alley, I didn't feel sad. I almost felt relief.'

The fox looked dubious and his vixen was clearly anxious to get going.

'I know you don't believe me,' Beau went on. 'And I understand why. But I want you to know this. There are bad humans. Just like there are bad animals. I've seen enough of both to have learned that, often the hard way. But there are good ones too. Very good ones. Just like there are good dogs.'

He had no idea if what he was saying was reaching them.

But suddenly none of that mattered anyway. As through the morning sky came another long baying of the horn. Closer this time. Much closer, and accompanied by a sound that put the foxes on high alert: a chorus of barks. There could be no doubt. The hounds were coming.

And they were coming quickly.

40

The vixen spoke anxiously to the fox and you didn't need to speak French to know what she wanted to do. And Beau couldn't blame her.

'Let us help you,' he barked, though both foxes were too full of panic for him to tell if they believed him. 'We could help you hide. Find a barn, a den, anything.'

The male looked incredulous. 'You think that would help? They'd sniff us out in seconds. They can dig. Destroy any hole we care to hide in.' The foxes started to run. Beau followed them. So did Mabel, begrudgingly.

'But there must be *something* we can do. Throw them off track. Point them in the wrong direction.'

The male didn't look back as he answered: 'You know and I know that won't happen. Even if I could trust you, which I don't, the hounds won't listen to you. They'll trust their own noses ahead of yours. And they do what their humans tell them. Always. They won't stop until they do. Until we're dead.'

'They're not all like that,' Beau said, exasperated.

'Oh yes, your Peggy! Then where is she now? Why is she not here? She may not be like the others yet . . . but she will be, it's just a matter of time. And then? Then you'll see.'

Beau could think of no reply, but the vixen said something

instead, between long gasping breaths. The foxes picked up their pace, but Beau realised it would be fruitless to go with them. A bigger group would only make them more visible on the horizon, an easier target.

'Good luck!' he yelled. 'Find shelter! We'll delay them as best as we can. I promise. Not all hounds are the same!'

He didn't know if the foxes heard him. They were streaking too fast across the field, setting it alight in a fiery amber flash.

'Bomber,' Beau shouted. 'Can you see how far away they are now?'

This was the sort of task Bomber relished, but before he could even take off, Mabel interjected. 'What on earth do you think you're doing?' she yelled, with an anger that Beau didn't understand.

'What do you mean?'

'How can you be so dense!' She was raging now. 'This is the crocodile situation all over again. Why do you never, ever learn?'

Beau was confused. 'Crocodile? How? It's nothing like it!'

'It is exactly the same. Back there, you wanted to set a crocodile free, despite the fact that it would eat you and anyone else who came into its path. And here we are again, a matter of hours later, with you putting yourself, and *us*, in the firing line!'

'It's nothing like that,' he protested. 'I'm just trying to help. And these aren't crocodiles coming over the hill. These are dogs, just like me. Maybe I can persuade them. Or fool them. Or both.'

Mabel was ready to explode. 'Did you not listen to a word those foxes said? They're not all wagging tails and tricks. They're hunters, trained to kill. And if you try to get in their way then they'll do the same to you!'

Beau thought about what she was saying as the baying of the hounds grew louder.

'Why do you only see the worst in things?'

'I do not!'

'You do. I'm a dunce, Bomber is vermin . . . even Wilf! That boy loves you more than anything else, yet you still can't even say that you miss him. What is the matter with YOU?'

'The day I accept a lecture from the likes of you will be the day I die,' Mabel spat. 'All you've said from the moment the bomb exploded in Balham is how you want to get to Peggy. *She needs me. She's sad. I can heal her.* Yet you then turn around and do everything in your power to get yourself killed before you're even in the same county as her! Well, I'm sick of it. Do you hear me? Sick of your "loyalty", sick of your stupidity, and sick of constantly being put in danger. I'm not putting myself through it any more. I . . . am . . . finished. Done. Gone.'

Mabel's declaration however, was not as finite as she might have wished.

'Er . . . I think it might be a bit late for that,' said Bomber, as he looked behind them. And he was right, as for the first time, the hounds swept into view, eating up the ground with a stealth that was terrifying.

They seemed to fill the horizon, sweeping down off the

hills, almost in formation, and although they had clearly spotted Beau and Mabel, they showed no signs of slowing.

'Oh, dog,' hissed Mabel. 'What have you done to us this time?'

She didn't have long to find out, as Beau's plan was trampled into the ground, the first of the hounds sweeping past them, not caring if they barged them on the way.

'Stop!' Beau barked wildly, not believing he could be so invisible to his own kind.

'Stop?!' Mabel spat, incredulous. 'Is that your plan?'

Sadly her sarcasm wasn't misplaced. No matter how loudly Beau barked, the hounds did not slow, let alone acknowledge him. In fact, they knocked both him and Mabel to the ground, trampling them underfoot if they fell into their path.

'I told you!' Mabel screamed. 'But would you listen? Would you?'

Beau was incredulous, yet true to his character, he refused to give up yet.

'Wrong way!' he yelled. 'You're going the wrong way.' It was a wonder he could think straight, let alone do what he did next: pulling himself to his feet and sprinting after them.

'Idiocy!' Mabel yelled. 'Simple straightforward idiocy!'

'He doesn't know any different,' shouted Bomber from above, who had sensibly stayed out of range. 'But we need to see it as a positive, not a fault.'

'Not a *fault*? The definition of insanity is making the same mistake again and again, and expecting a different result.'

As an argument, it was difficult to disagree with, even for Bomber. Yet he tried. 'I'm begging you, Mabel. Don't give up on him. Not yet. Not now. I mean, look at him. Look at what he's doing. He needs us now more than ever.'

'Do you honestly think those hellhounds are going to listen to me either?'

'Well, no, but we're stronger together. We're a . . .'

'If you *dare* compare us to an army, bird, I swear I will swallow you whole.'

'So if I don't say it, will you help? Please?'

Mabel looked at the ground, then at the stupid, ridiculous dog, still haring after the hounds. She shook her head, aghast at what she was about to say.

'I swear, that dog will be the death of me.'

And she took off in pursuit.

41

Beau was fighting a losing battle. The problem wasn't catching the hounds, the problem was getting them to hear him, or even acknowledge his existence.

'You've got it wrong!' he yelled. 'You're going in the wrong direction!'

As arguments went it was a lame one, and as Mabel finally caught up, she was able to tell him so.

'They're scent hounds, you fool!' she shouted. 'They're not going to believe you over their noses!'

'Then how do I make them stop?'

'How do *I* know? This is your plan, not mine.'

'But it's not working!'

Mabel couldn't disagree with that, but for once she didn't have a witty response either. Another cluster of hounds bore down on them, knocking them clean off their feet. The only difference this time was that two of the hounds fell with them, yelping as they rolled.

'What do you think you're *doing*?' one of them snarled, clearly seeing Mabel as the perpetrator.

Mabel went to protest her innocence, but she'd been right all along. These dogs were hunters. Killers. The first hound was already running, hunting the foxes, but the second simply pounced, jaws open, claws extended, enveloping Mabel in a flash.

Beau, pulling himself to his feet, couldn't see her beneath the hound's bulk, even when he circled it entirely.

'Get off her!' he barked. 'Leave her be!'

But the hound either couldn't or wouldn't listen, its jaws snapping left and right as it tossed Mabel around the furrowed field.

Bomber, spotting the turmoil, threw himself in the direction of the hound, but his beak couldn't serve as an effective deterrent. The beagle had locked on its prey and wouldn't stop until the job was done.

This left only Beau, who wrapped his own jaws onto the rump of the attacker in the hope of shocking him away. Beau felt his canines break the skin and waited for a yelp, a movement, or submission even, but when none of these came, he had no choice but to strengthen his grip, which still had no effect. He was running out of time.

Mabel yowled. A noise Beau had never heard from her or any other cat: a terrifying mixture of fear and pain that told him she had only seconds left. But what could he do? He'd used every weapon he owned. And then he heard Bomber holler from above.

'Beau, protect yourself! Now!'

He had no idea why, or how to do this effectively. But he did his best, releasing his teeth from the hound as a pack of horses announced themselves, thundering past, buffeting him this way and that.

Beau yelped, hooves catching his tail as he rolled. He saw steam coming off the horses' flanks, escaping from their nostrils. They were as single-minded as the dogs they were chasing. However, as the pack bounded on, one single horse and its rider turned back, and galloped towards the hound still on top of Mabel.

Oh Lord, panicked Beau. *If the beagle hasn't finished Mabel, the huntsman will.* He watched in horror as the man leaned sideways off his steed, whilst raising his whip high in the air.

Beau panicked. Both he and Bomber were too far away to intervene, and could only watch as the man's weapon came raining down . . . flat onto the back of the hound.

'What are you doing?' the man yelled, as the hound yelped in pain, dropping Mabel instantly. 'That's not a fox! It's a cat, you fool!'

The dog cowered, fearing a second blow from its master.

'Well, come on!' he yelled. 'What are you waiting for? That way!' and his whip pointed, to everyone's relief, in the direction of the rest of the pack, which sent the hound bounding on, desperate to please. To kill.

The two friends exhaled. It felt like they'd been holding their breath for hours. 'Mabel,' Beau stammered, 'is sh-sh-she all right?'

He dashed to her side, his body yelping in pain of its own.

Mabel's chest rose and fell. Each breath thin and rapid, each breath laced with pain.

Beau felt slightly easier that she was actually breathing, though she remained unresponsive, even when he nudged her onto her back.

'Come on now,' he implored. 'Enough play-acting.'

The cat did not reply.

'I said that's ENOUGH!' he growled. And nudged her again with his nose, harder this time. There was no riposte, no sarcastic barb, not even a snarl in disgust.

'Be gentle,' warned Bomber. 'She's really hurt, clearly. How much air she's actually getting into those lungs, well, I don't know, but it doesn't look like much.'

'So what do we do?'

'I'm not sure.'

Beau was aghast. It was the first time the bird didn't have a plan.

'How far is it to town? To Bournemouth.'

'Roughly? Five miles, maybe more.'

Beau surveyed the surroundings. It was uniformly empty of anyone or anything that could help.

'And if I move her, would that be bad?'

'Well, I don't think it would be good, do you?'

Beau looked down at the cat. There were areas of her body stripped bare of fur, with large bloody welts weeping as blood struggled to congeal. She couldn't stand, that was for sure. And Beau feared for how long she could fight off the cold. He had to make a decision, right there and then, so he pushed his muzzle into the back of Mabel's neck.

'What are you doing?' Bomber asked.

'Looking for a patch of skin where she isn't already bleeding.'

He looked on, sniffing all the while, until content that it was safe.

'This is all my fault,' he sniffed. 'I might as well have done this to her myself. So I need to put it right. I need to get her somewhere warm, and I need to do it now.'

Before the bird could argue or formulate a different plan, Beau found a scruff of fur and clenched it between his teeth, as though she were a kitten and he its mother. It took every bit of energy and effort he possessed to lift her, though. And when he took his first full stride, he realised the horses' hooves had trodden on more than just his tail. Fireworks of pain exploded in front of him with every step.

'Beau,' pleaded Bomber. 'I know you feel guilty. But you just can't do it. Look at you.'

Beau remained silent for obvious reasons, but he also chose to ignore Bomber's warning. The sense of blame engulfed him and only this could dilute it.

He closed one eye as he took the next step. It was somehow an improvement, but it took great willpower to keep his paws moving over the furrowed field.

Bomber flew above them, astonished. This was the stuff the older birds had spoken of, the bravery, the valour that war demanded, and it was happening right in front of his eyes.

'That's it, Beau,' he cooed encouragingly. 'You're doing it. Nearly there. I promise. If you can just keep going.'

Beau tried. He really did. He tried long after his energy ran out, after his body sobbed, then wailed, then screamed at him to stop and lie down. And the thing that kept him going? Through his one open eye, he swore he could see her. Peggy. She was there on the brow of the hill, all smiles and pigtails. Just as he remembered her.

She got closer, or he thought she did, which made him speed up, made the pain intensify too, so much so that his second eye closed too, just momentarily.

And when he opened it again? Peggy was gone. As was his hope.

To Bomber's horror, Beau collapsed to the ground, taking Mabel with him.

42

Beau saw a light in the corner of his eye. Blinding, flashing. Then nothing.

The light returned, accompanied by a loud flickering sound, like a thousand moths were flapping around it, but it faded the second his lids sagged shut.

The nothingness came and went, as did the moments in between, until finally, *finally,* his eyes stayed open long enough to see where he was.

A room. Inside. Warmth.

He was on a cushion, made of worn velvet, so comfortable that he had to fight to not give into sleep again. On his left there was a bowl of water, and beside that, another bowl, offering a mound of dry biscuits. The only problem was he daren't move to try them. Even lying still hurt.

So he moved his eyes instead, which kept the pain to a minimum. It was a smallish room, but its walls were covered in posters, a bright, tattered collage of smiling faces and exciting scenes. There were swordfights, vampires and pirates, a man hanging from the hands of a clock high up from the ground, as well as glamorous women with the fullest lips, and two men in bowler hats, one pencil thin, the other as ruddy as a butcher.

Beau had no idea where he was or what any of it meant, but for some strange reason, and despite his pain, he felt safe.

'Aye, aye,' said a voice from nowhere, 'look who's finally awake?'

It made Beau flinch, such was the shock of it, and the flinch brought a lightning bolt of pain flashing up his spine and into his head.

He tried to bark a single word, 'Mabel', but his mouth was so encrusted with blood and spittle that nothing came out but a low pathetic groan.

'Here,' said the voice, 'get yer tongue round this.' And a black, scarred muzzle pushed the water bowl closer still.

Beau didn't want to move, was scared to even try, but he needed to know where his friend was, that she was safe. He almost longed to hear her insult him. So with great effort, he lifted his head and dropped it over the side of the bowl, not caring that water spurted into his eyes and onto the floor. He drank. It tasted like the sweetest of elixirs.

A whine escaped his lips without him meaning it to, which prompted encouragement.

'Yer doing well,' said the voice. 'First water you've drunk by yourself in four days, that.'

Beau spluttered into the bowl.

'Four days?' He felt nausea and panic rise in him. 'How?'

'Bernard kept waking you up. Spooning it into your mouth, the best he could.'

But Beau wasn't worried about that. All he could think about was the four days.

It couldn't have been that long. Peggy? What about Peggy? His brain told him to get to his feet, and he tried, but his legs were not his own. It felt like the bones had been replaced with jelly, only this was painful, sore jelly. As soon as he applied any pressure to his limbs, he fell, knocking over both bowls and feeling not only defeated but humiliated too.

'Steady now,' came the voice again. It was gruff, but not unkind. 'Little wonder you can't stand, either of you. After what you've been through.'

Beau's ears rang with pain but he still heard the important bit, the bit that said 'either of you'.

'Mabel?' he said. 'Mabel's here? Mabel? Mabel?'

'Quiet now,' hushed the voice, which was attached to a craggy bulldog, whose face was a mess of folds and creases that even a mangle couldn't have straightened. 'There's a matinee on, and the projector room wall in't that thick! Mabel's in there with Bernard. The other dogs 'ere, well, some of 'em aren't so keen on cats, so he's keeping 'er safely tucked away.'

Beau tentatively looked around him to find a ragtag collection of dogs, all looking attentively at him. There was a black Lab, a spaniel with ears almost longer than its body, and others who were undoubtedly mongrels like Beau.

A healthier, less pained Beau would've pointed out that maybe these dogs should've been fearful of *Mabel*, but he was so exhausted, and so relieved to hear that the cat had made it too, that he said and did nothing. Instead, he let his head fall beside the water bowl and allowed sleep to pull him under.

He woke later, much later, given the change of light in the room, and managed to sweep up the biscuits that he'd spilled on the floor. The food didn't help.

If anything, it only served to make him sleepy again, a tiredness that overwhelmed him and left him powerless to do anything but obey.

The next time Beau came to, there was a man leaning over him, which made him initially fearful, muscles tensing despite the discomfort this brought with it.

'Hey now,' whispered the man, his open palm soothing Beau behind the ears. 'Don't fret.' He continued to stroke Beau, before lifting a tube with his other hand. 'Now listen 'ere, this might sting a little bit, but the vet says I've got to put it on you three times daily. Them cuts of yours were dirty. Not as dirty as the cat's, though. Screamed blue murder, she did, when I first put it on.'

This was not a surprise to Beau, and he didn't envy the man the job of playing nurse to Mabel. It felt like the least he could do was not make a fuss, so he lay there, as still as he could, only tensing when the man's fingers touched upon a particularly infected spot.

'There you go,' said the man finally. 'You were lucky. The both of you. A few more hours, and the vet says it might have been too late. So rest now. The vet's given me some more delights for you, but I'll sort the cat out first. I'll be back later, if she doesn't scratch me to death first.'

The man said it with a wry grin and soft chuckle that clearly told Beau he had not only worked Mabel out, but that he could be trusted. They would be safe here.

Each time he woke and ate, Beau stayed awake a little longer. The man returned with his smile and his medicine, and Beau spent the time filling in the gaps of how he'd made it from the middle of a field, to here.

'Some bloke found you,' he was told by Monty, the dog he'd met when he first awoke. 'Walking his spaniel, he was. Wasn't sure if the cat was even breathing at first. His spaniel refused to leave you. Whined and fussed until he brought you here, to us.'

Beau was grateful to the man and his dog, whoever and wherever they were, but he still had questions.

'What about Bomber?' he asked. He couldn't see him anywhere.

'Bomber? Who's Bomb— Oh, the bird? Don't be worrying about him. He appeared on that window ledge the day you arrived, and didn't budge all the time you were asleep. Been freezing out there too. Howling wind and rain, but he stuck it out. Proper soldier, that one.'

Beau would've laughed if it hadn't been so painful.

'So where is he now?'

'Gone to have a look at something. 'cept he didn't call it that. Called it a reconnaissance mission, whatever that is. He'll be back. That bit I did understand.'

Beau felt a blinding sense of relief, but still didn't know why they'd been brought to this place.

'Cos of Bernard, of course,' Monty answered. '*Saint* Bernard, we call him, which is ironic in't it, given how many dogs live here, and he's the only one who's human.'

Beau was none the wiser.

'Let me explain,' said Monty. 'Bernard Woolley, Saint Bernard, he runs this place. The cinema. Has done for years. And he's always had a dog, see, two sometimes. So when war broke out, and the government told people to have their animals put to sleep, lots of 'em refused. But they was too scared or ashamed to be seen going against what Chamberlain instructed. Instead they started dumping 'em. Hard to believe, I know. But Bernard, well, he couldn't just turn a blind eye. So if he found a dog, he took it in. Then word got out and suddenly dogs were being left tied to the railings next to the box office. Before he knew it, old Bernard's got a whole cast of us living here.'

'How many?'

'There was at least twenty at one point. 'Cept that got a bit much. Poor old bloke could barely afford to eat cos he was feeding us instead. He didn't do what the others did, mind.

214

No one was put to sleep or abandoned. He found homes for 'em instead, which was no small feat given what Hitler's been up to.'

'So how many live here now?'

'Six. It's still enough, mind. With you, in fact it's seven. Plus the cat.'

'Where does everyone sleep?'

'Wherever there's space. In the auditorium when there in't a film showing, and if there is, well the only rule is we keep quiet. Folks can't follow the story if there's howling going on. And if Saint Bernard don't sell tickets, then we don't eat. When you understand it like that, it's easy for everyone to keep it zipped.'

'Well, it'll be a bit quieter very soon, cos me and Mabel will have to get moving. Once Bomber's back, we'll be on our way.' Beau went to stand and failed miserably.

'Come on, now. You don't have to prove to me that you're a brave one. I can see that, plain as day. But you aren't going nowhere, not right now. And neither is that cat. Hell of a state she was in. Like she'd fought with a wolf. Or a pack of 'em. She wouldn't make it down the stairs right now, never mind to this lighthouse the pigeon was talking about.'

'But she'll be all right, won't she?'

'I'm no vet, but I don't think it'll happen overnight.'

'It doesn't matter. Long as she's alive. She needs Wilf just like I need Peggy. So we'll wait for her,' he said, decisively.

'That's the spirit,' offered Monty. 'And besides, you haven't spent time with Saint Bernard yet. Few hours in his company and you'll never want to leave.'

Beau tried to wag his tail but it hurt. He was sure Bernard was indeed a saint, but all he could think of was Mabel, the lighthouse and Peggy.

43

Monty wasn't wrong about Bernard. The man truly *was* a saint, albeit a wiry one. There was little wonder he was so thin, with the dogs to walk every day, never mind the constant scurrying around the picture house.

He was in his late forties, with slick, Brylcreemed hair like many of the suave men on his posters. He wore a thin, meticulously crafted moustache, which clung to his top lip, above a cigarette that burned constantly in his mouth.

He dressed smartly for a man with so many excitable, often grubby dogs jumping up at him. He had black and white spats on his feet, and pristine tailored trousers accompanied by a pair of braces that had to work extra hard to hold them up. The look was topped off by a white shirt and black tie, and if the cinema was open, a tweed suit jacket, complete with a flower in his buttonhole.

He never raised his voice or displayed any manner of exasperation towards the dogs in his care and showed them an unlimited amount of love. He was everything those hunters on horseback would never be, and Beau shivered at the thought of what they had bred their hounds to do.

Bernard seemed to revel in his local celebrity, nodding at folks on the street as his army of dogs walked beside him to the park for their daily exercise. Beau started to join them to build up his strength and they were never dull affairs, in fact, they were enormous fun. The Labrador, who answered to 'Rufus', definitely had an eye for the ladies. He was an obedient boy on the leash, but as soon as a lady dog took his eye in the park, he became deaf to Bernard, his attention solely on his new amour.

'He's watched too many romances back at the cinema, that one,' Monty told Beau. 'Thinks he's Errol Flynn. Look at him!'

Monty was right. The female dogs in the park would swoon over Rufus as soon as he wagged his tail in their direction, and despite Bernard indulging him the time to woo, the Lab always looked distraught when his master finally dragged him home.

The other dogs were nowhere near as amorous. All they needed, Beau included, was a ball to be thrown for them on repeat. It didn't matter how many times Bernard hurled it, they would chase endlessly, even Monty, whose short legs gave him the cruellest of disadvantages. To Beau, it felt good: a relief that he was on the mend, though he did feel pangs of guilt as he tore around the park. This was something he should be doing with Peggy, not a stranger.

Back at the picture house, Mabel barely moved at all, and certainly had no desire to be close to the other dogs.

'Once bitten, twice shy,' she said, without a hint of sarcasm.

Beau had been surprisingly pleased to be reunited with her,

but he put it down to the overwhelming guilt he felt at getting her into such a damaged state. He apologised more than once, but she never really acknowledged it. She acknowledged very little, lying on the cushion in Bernard's office, her nose turned away from food, water and conversation, even if that meant missing opportunities to rub Beau's nose in it.

'I've lost count of the number of times you've saved me now,' he said to her, waiting for the barbed reply. But none came back.

It worried him. He gave her other chances to ridicule him in the hope of cheering her up, but each one was ignored, leaving Beau desperately thinking of other ways to engage her.

She did not look well. Despite Saint Bernard's nursing, her cuts and grazes were many, with one in particular on her front right leg, which still oozed pus.

'That one is definitely infected,' he offered. 'You should try licking it too, to keep it clean.'

Mabel didn't move or even look at her wound.

'I could lick it for you, if you like?' He paused, thinking of a quip she wouldn't resist replying to. 'Mind you, you don't know where my tongue's been, eh?'

Her reply could be as caustic as she wished. He didn't mind. But her mouth didn't move. The only thing that did were her eyes, closing gently.

'Mabel?' Beau said, gently. 'Mabel, I'm worried about you. I'm worried you're not yourself. I'm worried you're more hurt than you're letting on.'

One eye opened, just a touch, before closing again.

'And I need you to be well, you know. Because . . . we can't go without you, can we?'

He hoped *this* would elicit a response, but it didn't work, which made his heart sink, his own eyes closing not in tiredness, but worry.

'I'm not coming any further.' Her words weren't loud, but they were clear.

Beau's eyes shot open. 'What?'

'I said I'm not coming.'

Beau sat upright, tense. 'But you have to.'

'No, I don't.' Her eyes were still closed.

'But we need you.'

'I'm tired, dog. I can't talk about this any more. When you leave, I'll stay here. Build up my strength, then head for home. It's for the best.'

Beau couldn't believe what he was hearing. 'For the best? Best for who? Because it's not the best for Wilf, that's for sure. That boy needs you. And I think you need him too.'

Silence. Not a flicker of a response.

'You won't be happy back in Balham,' Beau went on. 'There might be mice there, and rats. But you can't love something and eat it too. You'll be all on your own and you won't like it in the end. You won't. You might be a cat, but cats get lonely too.'

Mabel's eyes opened and she pushed herself onto straight front legs, wincing as she did it.

She looked at Beau. He looked back, then watched, helpless, as she turned away from him, and laid back down on the cushion.

The conversation, and more importantly, Mabel's involvement in the mission, appeared to be over.

44

A small break in the clouds appeared when Beau was woken by an incessant tapping on the window. Bomber had returned, his chest seeming to glow brighter than ever, despite the gloom.

Beau padded happily over to the draughty old window and managed to nudge it ajar to allow his friend to bounce in.

'I'm happy to see you on your feet,' Bomber cooed.

'Thanks. I'm feeling a lot stronger now. It's Mabel we should be worried about.'

'I know.'

'You do?'

'Of course. I've flown back and forth over the last few days, but when I've looked through her window, she's always been asleep.'

'Back and forth? From where?'

'The lighthouse, of course. Anvil Point.'

Beau's ears pricked up. 'You found it?'

'Of course.' Bomber looked almost affronted at the suggestion that he might not have.

'And did you see her. My Peggy?'

There was a pause, an awkward silence where Bomber's proud chest seemed to deflate a little.

'I did,' he said, before changing the subject. 'What's the problem with Mabel? Is she not on the mend?'

Beau felt torn. Who did he talk about first? 'Mabel's a little better, I suppose. But she says she's not coming any further. Says she's going home.'

'She *what?* And miss out, when we're so close?'

'That's what I said to her. Maybe you should try. She might listen to you. Anyway, what about Peggy? She's not hurt, is she?'

There was another pause. 'Well, no. Not physically.'

'What do you mean?'

'I'm sorry, Beau. But Peggy and Wilf . . . they know about their parents.'

Beau was stunned. It was not the news he wanted to hear.

A whimper escaped him.

'I'm sorry, Beau. I really am. But you mustn't feel bad that you weren't there to comfort her. It only happened yesterday. A telegram came, you see.'

'And what did she say? What happened?'

'Honestly?'

Beau nodded.

'She didn't say much, not that I could hear from the window ledge outside, anyway. But there were tears of course. Lots of them.'

'And since then?'

'The same really. She's been outside a little. But on her own. Thinking, weeping. Wilf hasn't even stepped outside the house.'

Beau felt his own heart break. He should've been there when she needed him. He'd let her down in a way that she never would've and he didn't know if he could forgive himself.

'I tried to cheer her up, Beau, best I could. I swooped and circled, did a great Spitfire impression and everything, but to be honest I don't think she realised I was there. Not surprising, really.'

But Beau hadn't heard what Bomber said. His ears were too full of his own regret and shame. He needed to be with her. More than ever. But he also knew that Wilf would need Mabel. And that may prove to be more than a little problematic.

45

More than ever, Beau and Bomber needed a plan.

But as the plan involved changing Mabel's mind, it needed to be their finest yet. Greater, more strategic minds than theirs could've tried and failed, but they couldn't let that deter them.

Early attempts were obvious and gentle, Bomber announcing his reappearance, waxing lyrical about the coastline they were heading to.

'Rats and the mice the size of small dogs down there,' he enthused. 'You'll never be hungry again, I swear.'

This didn't tempt Mabel's eyes to even flutter, never mind open.

'Poor Wilf looked very sad, though. Barely moved from the sofa while I was watching. There was actually a perfect cat-sized spot next to him. Raging fire, too.'

At that, Mabel turned her head away from them, resolutely, leaving Bomber no option but to try a more sergeant-majorly approach.

'Now you listen to me, soldier. I know we took a pasting out there on the fields, and I know your wounds are not insignificant. But look how far we've come. And think about how close the lighthouse is now. You're not going to give that up now, are you?'

Mabel seemed to sigh especially deeply but still didn't rouse herself, leaving Bomber with what he thought was his last option.

'That's not a request, soldier. There's a family down there, grieving. A little boy needing his cat more than he ever has before. So whatever you're feeling, shake it off, get on your feet and think about something other than yourself for once. THAT is an ORDER.'

Finally, Mabel turned her head, eyes opening lazily. 'When are you going to learn, bird, that you are not a soldier, and neither am I? The only things you are going to be, if you keep on bothering me, is A, in pain, and then B, my lunch. If that's your mission, then please, carry on.'

Bomber may have been brave, but he was also pragmatic, and chose to beat a sensible retreat to devise a new plan (and preserve his plumage).

'Your turn,' he said to Beau, who had even less success than his friend.

'I don't know why you're bothering,' said Monty, as he watched the pair. 'I mean, I know that cat ain't well, but if she don't want to go, leave her. Simple, ain't it?'

'It should be,' said Beau. 'After all, she's said she didn't want to come, right from the off.'

'There you go then. Simple.'

'But,' said Beau, 'I've never believed her. You never saw

her with Wilf. She was different with him. On his lap, round his legs. She loved him. She never admitted it, probably never will, but she did. I'm telling you.'

'So why's she quitting now?'

Beau shrugged, he only wished he knew. Because until he did, he wouldn't be able to change Mabel's mind.

Exercise helped, in some ways. With every walk he took alongside Saint Bernard, or every lap of the auditorium he strode, Beau felt his strength return, as well as his will to finish the journey. It intensified his conflict though, without doubt.

He could see Mabel's physical health improving. The food in her bowl was disappearing, as was her water, and she wasn't always to be found on her cushion either. Perhaps she was exercising too, Beau thought.

She still wouldn't hear of rejoining the mission, though, and Beau knew that his time and influence were quickly running out.

'Take your mind off it, for Pete's sake,' said Monty. 'Saint Bernard will be starting the film any minute. Laurel and Hardy tonight. It'll be a hoot.'

Beau doubted there was anything that could lighten his mood, but he did as he was told, sitting with the other dogs at the open window of the projector room, as Bernard rolled the newsreel, a grainy shot of Big Ben giving Beau a pang of homesickness.

'Right, you lot,' Bernard said. 'Behave yourselves for five

minutes while I make myself a cuppa,' and he strode from the room, as the newsreader on the screen began.

'*London,*' he said. '*The potential jewel in Hitler's crown. Yet if Adolf wants to take not just our capital city, but the spirit of its residents, then he's going to have to work an awful lot harder!*' The footage cut to full buses and pavements, as people bustled to work.

Monty was slightly confused. ''Ere,' he said. 'I thought you two said London was being flattened night after night?'

'It is,' Beau replied. 'You should've seen Balham High Road.'

'Well, apart from the sandbags, you wouldn't even know there was a war on!'

Beau frowned. Monty had a point, and he hadn't a clue what the answer was.

'They're hardly going to show the damage Hitler's done, are they?' said Bomber.

'You mean they're hiding it? On purpose?'

'Well, of course they are. I mean, what's it going to do for morale across the country if all people see is death and destruction?'

'Not a lot,' the bulldog replied.

'Exactly. This war could last months yet. Years. So the government need to keep people smiling. If they can. Or at the very least, confident that the Nazis aren't getting through.'

Beau sat and watched the news roll on, but as that report ended, he caught sight of movement in the auditorium below. It wasn't a latecomer. Not a human one anyway, as there was no mistaking the prowl of Mabel, as she slinked unnoticed onto a seat towards the back. There was a slow fluidity to her movements that surprised Beau. She didn't look back to full health, but not far off.

'See who's watching?' Beau whispered to Bomber. 'Maybe it would be better if she saw the damage in Balham up there on screen? Might make her change her mind?'

But this was wishful thinking, as instead, the next report took in rolling fields and valleys, as the reporter continued.

'*It's over a year now since trains swept the first of our brave young evacuees to their new homes in the countryside. And more than a million and a half lucky boys and girls have been given a glimpse into a life that they may not otherwise have seen, even if they lived to be a hundred.*'

This was the cue for footage of happy children, skipping through school gates, listening intently to lessons.

'*No lessons have been missed, no homework left unfinished. In fact, our children are learning things they could never have been exposed to in our cities.*'

Beau watched as children now walked through rich grassy fields, chasing collies as they rounded sheep. Others carried slopping pails of milk from barns or cradled newborn lambs in their arms.

Beau wondered if Wilf and Peggy had felt as happy as these children, before they heard the news about their parents. A final shot flashed up on screen of a small, grubby-faced boy, tenderly cuddling a cat, and Beau was suddenly aware of Mabel's reaction. The second the child appeared on screen,

Mabel did the strangest thing. She bolted. Literally jumped from the seat and ran, seemingly unimpeded, out of the auditorium.

The only time Beau had seen her react in such a way was when she was nearly eaten by a crocodile. So he knew that Mabel was scared. And he realised that if he wanted her to rejoin their mission, then he had to find out why.

46

Beau found Mabel in the foyer, still unusually agitated.

'Are you all right?' he asked innocently, as if happening on her accidentally.

'Perfect. No thanks to *you*.'

Beau let it slide. 'It's just . . . well . . . I saw you leave the film. You looked . . . unhappy.'

'Don't be ridiculous. I mean – what on earth do I have to be unhappy about? It's not like I'm a hundred miles from home with a body that's been damaged and broken, is it?'

Beau decided to be brave.

'You didn't look too damaged when you dashed out of the auditorium. The only thing that looked pained was your face.'

'How kind, given the attractiveness of your own.'

'That's not what I meant. I think you ran out because of what you saw on the screen.'

There was a fleeting moment of indecision before Mabel feigned interest in a stain on the carpet at her feet, scratching and sniffing it intently.

'Mabel?'

'What?'

'That boy. Hugging the cat. It upset you, didn't it? Or rather, it scared you.'

'Scared me?' She lifted her head, eyes wide with indignation. 'Piffle.'

'Oh, you can deny it all you want. But I know what I saw.'

'You really are quite the detective, aren't you?' Mabel scoffed, but Beau knew there was truth in his words.

'So what's going on? That boy holding a cat, that's the same way Wilf held you a thousand times. You were only ever affectionate when he cuddled you. So why, when you're so close to having all that back again, would you possibly turn and run for home? What are you afraid of?'

'It's none of your business!'

'Maybe not. But I've had you speak your mind to me every day for the past year, so I think I've earned the right today. You're scared. Admit it!' Beau barked more loudly than he meant to. 'Admit it! And tell me why! Tell me . . . the truth!'

'Because you're not the only one who's had to live on the streets!' cried Mabel.

'What?'

'All I've heard,' Mabel said, voice laced with rare emotion, 'all I've ever heard, since you arrived, is how you were homeless. How you were mistreated. How awful it was. Did you ever stop to think that you might not be the only one?'

Beau had a number of issues with what Mabel had said. He was *not* one to seek or wallow in sympathy, but it seemed unimportant at that moment.

'What do you mean? *You?*'

'Yes, me!' Mabel said, indignant. 'I had a life *before* you wormed your way in.'

'So tell me then.'

'Why bother? I'm sure whatever happened to me wasn't a patch on your sob story.'

'That's nonsense and you know it.'

'No, what's nonsense is your ridiculous belief that your girl, your beloved Peggy, will still love you when you get there.'

'It's not nonsense.'

'Lord, you're stupid. Look at what's happened since we left. Hasn't that taught you anything? Attacked by rats. Mauled by a crocodile. Set on by your own kind, for pity's sake, then left to die in a field by their owners. How can you trust anyone?'

'Because those children are special and they love us.'

'They *did*.'

'They still do!'

'You don't know that for sure, and I definitely don't. People . . . change. Their minds, their behaviour. They say one thing and do another.'

'That's not true. Wilf worships you.'

Mabel exhaled deeply, then paused, as if what she was about to say was getting stuck on her tongue. 'And so did the boy before him.'

'Before Wilf?'

'That's right. He was no different. He wanted me. Played

with me, let me sleep on his bed. I was his everything, until . . . I wasn't.'

'What do you mean?'

'Exactly that. He lost interest. Fell out of love. Found something different. And as soon as he did that, his parents saw no point in having me around either. Why feed something that served no purpose?'

'But that boy, well, he's not Wilf, is he?'

Mabel shook her head. 'He's not, but he could be. Humans are fickle. So if I'm going to go back to Balham, and go back to living on the street, well, that's going to be my choice. Not someone else's.'

'Then you will live a sad life.'

'Nonsense, I've not met a rodent I couldn't catch.'

'Being full doesn't equal being happy.' Beau wasn't going to let Mabel have the final word. Not this time. 'You might be scared, but so am I. So is Bomber. None of us know what's going to happen, not just when we reach the lighthouse, but in between. That doesn't mean we should run away from it.

'We have to take risks and believe that it'll be all right in the end. Because I'm telling you, cat, that if the end of the world does happen, and that boy doesn't come running to you, well, you'll still be breathing, and the world will still be turning, and you still won't be on your own. Because there will be Bomber. And there will be me. If we were going to disown you, we'd have done it ages ago.'

Beau's attempt at humour fell flat, but Mabel did not fight back.

'We're going to leave for the lighthouse tomorrow,' he said. 'When the matinee starts. We really want you to come with us.'

And with that, he walked away to rest.

47

It felt ungrateful to leave the picture house without thanking Saint Bernard properly, but they had no choice. Beau hoped that he would understand, be relieved in a way as he would have fewer mouths to feed.

The thing that really occupied his mind, however, was whether Mabel would choose to join them.

He hadn't spoken to her again on this or any other subject. He'd let her be, choosing to garner every bit of strength he would need for the last leg of the journey.

'We should be on our way,' said Bomber from the window ledge. 'While Bernard is loading the projector.'

Beau nodded. There was no sign of Mabel, even as he made his way quietly to the rear exit of the cinema, where he bade farewell to Monty.

Come on, Beau mouthed to himself. *Where are you?*

The answer lay on the other side of the door, as there stood not just Bomber, but Mabel too.

'The matinee started two minutes ago,' she said, utterly deadpan. 'Typical lax behaviour, from a typically lax mutt.' And without another word, she turned and walked on.

Beau's jaw hit the ground. Where was the vulnerability, the honesty, the uncertainty she'd shown only the day before?

'Say nothing, soldier,' whispered Bomber supportively. 'She's with us. Mission accomplished. Onwards.'

They made good progress, with Bomber navigating as usual. It was noticeable that the bird made frequent pauses at various junctions. Beau knew exactly what that was about: Bomber wasn't lost (as if), he was merely allowing Mabel a little time to rest and recuperate without her noticing.

Bournemouth was a lovely town, though out of season the pavements stood eerily empty at times. The arcades and penny slots were closed, their once-bright lights dull and dusty. The only raucous signs of life came from the seagulls that cawed and wailed, their voices bouncing off the buildings in a way that felt almost sinister.

The road the trio followed next hugged the sea itself, long and straight, and Beau made himself imagine Peggy standing at the end of it.

It's all right, Beau thought, *she's there. I know it.*

'See that spit of land sticking out into the sea?' Bomber told them. 'That's Sandbanks, where the ferry leaves from.'

'Ferry?' said Mabel. It was the first word she'd uttered since they'd left the picture house.

'That's right. But it doesn't go far, just across the estuary to Studland. From there it's a hop, skip and a jump down to Anvil Point, I promise.'

'Would it not be safer for us to follow the land round instead of getting the ferry?'

'Safer, maybe,' said Bomber matter-of-factly, 'but infinitely longer. Follow that route and we add another twenty miles at least.'

'I vote the ferry,' Beau said quickly.

'Me too,' added Bomber. 'And besides, it will give us all a chance to recharge our batteries.' Beau liked the sound of that, but knew Bomber wasn't referring to himself. He could fly to Africa if he so chose.

Mabel scowled and made a noise that sat somewhere between a hiss and sigh. In cat terms, it was clearly a curse on them all, but for once she toed the line, falling in behind them.

48

When they reached the end of the coastal road, a line of vans, carts and cars stood between them and the estuary. Some of them carried soldiers.

'Army onboard that one,' Beau said, grateful for the chance to rest.

'Air Force,' Bomber corrected. 'Canadian. A fine, brave bunch. There's a base over the water at Worth Matravers.'

'You should go and sit on the bonnet of their truck,' said Mabel. 'Be a good boy and you could be their mascot. Maybe then finally they'll make a soldier of you.'

'*Make* me a soldier?' He looked bemused. 'They are magnificent, but I don't need their help. My time is coming, don't you worry.'

'Of course it is,' sighed Mabel. 'How silly of me.'

Bomber had already moved on, darting into the sky for a minute before returning with his next order.

'Follow me,' he whispered, leaving no space for insubordination as he led them closely alongside the vehicles' wheels.

'What are you doing?' Mabel hissed.

'Finding you safe passage. I very much doubt they allow lippy cats onboard.'

He flew on, until he reached an open-bed cart, pulled by a huge carthorse. It did not seem delighted to be there, little wonder, as the load it was pulling was immense, and smelled indescribably bad.

'What is that?' Mabel moaned as her stomach turned.

'Manure.'

'Manure?'

'Yes, you know, animal waste—'

'I know what animal waste is, strangely. I just don't understand why you're leading us so close to it.'

'Because there's space for both of you to hide amongst it till we cross the estuary.'

'I'd rather die,' said Mabel.

'Well, stay here overnight and you might well do that. Do you know how cold it gets when the sun goes down?'

'I'm guessing pretty chilly?'

Beau had heard enough. They had to cross this water to get to where they needed to be, and that was enough for him. So he pulled himself onboard, positioning himself in a postage stamp-sized space where the floor was relatively clean.

'Filthy, filthy beast,' smirked Mabel, which made Beau bite his tongue. 'I shall see you on the other side.' And without a backwards glance, she slinked to the Canadians' truck and leaped straight onto an airman's lap, looking up with adoring eyes.

She was, of course, an instant hit, and welcomed every bit of adulation and titbit thrown her way. Beau was pretty sure he could see her laughing at him. Still, he was safe, and getting closer and closer to Peggy.

He took the time to rest as Bomber stood watch from the cart's wall. The smell was strong, but he didn't mind it, and as the cart rumbled and rolled onboard the ferry, the vibrations eased his weary bones.

'Will it be a long journey?' Beau asked. He'd never been on a boat and didn't much care for the thought of it.

'So short, you'll hardly notice. We won't be out at sea, and there is no chance of us being blown offshore either.'

'How do you mean?'

'It's a chain ferry.'

'A what-what?' He didn't mind sounding uneducated with Mabel out of earshot.

'Chain ferry.'

'Oh right,' he said, trying to look relieved. He paused. 'And what's that, then?'

'Well, it's a ferry that runs on a chain. Now, I'm no engineer, but I believe there's a long chain that runs along the bottom of the seabed, and it's attached to the boat. The chain keeps it on course and on time.'

'Oh. Right.' It all sounded pretty implausible, but so did the idea of dropping bombs on each other until one side won, and humans seemed to be managing that with no problem either. 'Will it get us closer to Peggy?'

'It will.'

'Then I like chain ferries,' Beau said, and he rested his head on his front paws as the ferry roared into life.

It was a strange sensation, but not one that Beau would allow to disturb him. He could hear the water lapping then parting, and feel the rumble and groan of the chain as it slithered its way along the belly of the boat. As he looked to the side of the vessel and the view moved with him, he felt a swell of optimism. It was getting colder and darker but his destination was getting closer. And that was all that mattered.

49

'What is that *smell*?' gasped Mabel, though she knew full well where it was coming from.

Beau tried to ignore her, his attention focused on moving his legs, which were a little stiff after the time spent on the ferry.

'Excellent restraint.' Bomber congratulated Beau as the cat strode on. 'Nothing matters but those children.'

Beau knew that, felt it in every cell of his being, but he carried the weight of it too.

'Can I be honest with you, Bomber?' he said.

'You can.'

'It's not just Mabel feeling it. I'm scared too.'

'You're what? Come on now. You're nearly there.'

'I know. But what if when we get there, I can't do anything? What if I can't make it all better?'

Bomber landed in front of his friend, causing him to stop.

'You can't change what has already happened,' he said.

'I know that.'

'Then you're already halfway there. Tell me, when Peggy saved you from that van, did she take away all the other bad things that had happened to you?'

'Well, no.'

'And were you angry with her about that?'

'Angry? Why on earth would I be angry? None of it was her fault.'

'Exactly!' Bomber said emphatically. 'Just as what happened to her parents, as much as it pains you, that wasn't *your* fault either.'

'I don't know,' Beau replied, finding it hard to look Bomber in the eye. 'I could've warned Mr Alford. Should've pulled him away from the edge of that bloomin' hole.'

'And while you were at it, maybe you could've caught the bomb as it landed and thrown it back into space.' Bomber paused. 'Look at me, Beau. Look at me. This is important. Please.'

Beau did so, reluctantly.

'I'm going to say something to you now, and you mustn't take it the wrong way.' He took a deep breath. 'You're just a dog, Beau. A dog. You're a mighty dog, a loyal, kind, brave dog. You've saved dozens of lives with that nose of yours for goodness' sake. But you're still a dog. And a dog can't stop an entire army. Do you honestly think that when Peggy sees you, the first thing she'll feel is anger that you let her parents die?'

Beau shuffled from paw to paw. 'No. No, I don't think so.'

'No, I don't either. All that girl will feel is joy. Joy that you are alive and that you travelled, Lord knows how, all that way, fighting rats and horses and hounds and a crocodile for Pete's sake. And yes, that joy will be replaced by the pain again, but the difference will be that you'll be next to her. You'll hold it for her, in exactly the same way she did for you. She never took away the pain of what happened to you, but she made it easier to carry. And that's all you need to do for her.'

Beau didn't know what to say, so he tried to say thank you, but even then, the words came out as a mush of sound.

'You're welcome,' said Bomber, straightening his wings. 'Now come on. This mission is not over. Not yet.'

He took to the skies with minimum effort and Beau watched as he soared in front of him. He was some bird, that Bomber.

50

Darkness grew. And with it, tiredness.

But the three of them did not stop.

'It's a shame you're not seeing this in daylight, as I have,' Bomber told them. 'Studland Beach is rather beautiful. With the sun on it, it's the colour of gold. Twenty-four carats.'

Beau made himself imagine it. He looked at the shadows of the gorse and heather, at the sand beyond it, and then three miles later he could just make out Corfe Castle. There it sat, proudly on the top of a hill, its edges crumbling into shadow as night fell.

'So nearly there. Don't you dare stop now,' said Bomber, swooping from above. The village of Ulwell came and went in a blur: Beau didn't even bother to lift his head and look at it. What was the point? The thing, the person he wanted and needed, wasn't there. He barely even twitched when they hit Swanage either, despite it being a beautiful town, with an arcing bay and a crescent of beautiful pillared buildings. In the background, Beau heard the long smoky toot of a locomotive's horn, and whilst it reminded him of how their journey had started, it seemed such a long, long time ago that it felt almost like another life altogether.

As Swanage shrank behind them, it started to rain heavily.

'This is most unwelcome,' sighed Mabel. 'And had you been a larger, more imposing dog, you might at least have sheltered me a little.'

Beau ignored her and made himself take in the positives.

He allowed the rain to fall on his tongue, and it felt far from unpleasant, though after another twenty minutes or so, it did start to sit heavier upon his fur, until that became waterlogged, sliding from him like a waterfall.

He kept his eyes in front of him, though he couldn't help but be drawn to the sea on occasion. Sometimes it was the crash of an unexpectedly large wave that shocked him: the wind was picking up, driving the water harder and faster to shore. But finally, as the moon managed to cut momentarily through a cloud, he saw something else. A series of large oval balloons hovering above the coastline. They seemed incongruous, and it shocked him, though he had seen plenty of barrage balloons tethered around the Thames in London.

'What are they doing here?' he asked Bomber. 'It's not like there's houses to be protected round here, not really.'

'Well, if this is the first piece of England those bombers see, then they need to know they're not welcome: that we're going to protect ourselves. If they want to get to us, then they have to make it past the balloons first. In fact, look closer and you'll see it's not just the balloons standing guard.'

Beau looked, eyes scouring the gorse-filled land between them and the sea, and eventually, he found them: a series of barriers built from sandbags. Five or six of them were spread across the horizon, and from each protruded the biggest gun Beau had ever seen.

'What on earth are they?' Beau said. Even Mabel stopped to look.

'Ack Acks,' replied Bomber, matter-of-factly. 'Flak cannons. See either side of the gun there? There's seats for soldiers to sit, to weigh it down, then a third soldier stands in the middle to load the shells.'

'I wouldn't want to be on the receiving end of that,' gulped Beau.

'It's sights like that that make me proud to be a soldier,' admitted Bomber. 'When you think of the bravery it must take to sit there as an enemy plane thunders over.'

'I'm not sure your weight would add much to holding it to the ground,' sneered Mabel.

'I'd be airborne by then anyway,' replied Bomber, immune to her sarcasm. 'Where I was trained to be.'

'Of course you would,' the cat sighed. And she walked on, leaving Beau to stand and stare. He didn't like it, these weapons being so close to Peggy. He'd thought that out here, there'd be no sign of the war. Just fields or playgrounds and innocence. But here it was, lining the seafront, plain as day.

'Get us there, Bomber,' he said, feeling the rain pelt harder on his fur. 'Soon as you can.'

But as he said it, he heard a rumble in the distance.

'Is that thunder?' he asked. But no, he didn't think it was.

He listened again. It was growing louder.

Beau didn't like it. A shiver rippled through him. He turned to Bomber, who looked equally concerned.

'I know,' he said, quietly. 'I hear it too. We'd best get moving, Beau. They're coming. In fact, they'll soon be here.'

51

Beau didn't think he had ever moved so quickly in his life, keeping the tip of Bomber's tail mere inches in front of him.

It was a noise he had heard too many times in the past year, and he cursed himself for not recognising it sooner. *Thunder?* What on earth had he been thinking? No, this was enemy aircraft.

'Don't worry about it,' shouted Bomber, reading his mind. 'It makes no difference. The lighthouse is a mile ahead, two at most. Think of nothing but that.'

Beau nodded his agreement and pushed harder. He watched as Bomber dropped back a touch, presumably to encourage a flagging Mabel. The only thing that mattered was reaching those children. But what if the bombers targeted the lighthouse, Beau thought in horror. What if they wanted to knock out its beam and missed, taking out everything else around it?

The noise grew louder, the rain fell harder, even the wind had decided to join in, driving the drops at a deadly angle so they speared into Beau's face, making it hard to keep his eyes open more than a jot.

He fell, then a second time, each fall sapping his energy

but not his desire. It wasn't happening, he wasn't quitting now, but as the tiredness drove his disorientation, it finally came: help, a sign, call it what you will, but from out of nowhere, Anvil Point lighthouse flickered into view. It might only have been a dim beam, but it still scythed across the sky, sporadically lighting the space between Beau and his girl.

But the beam also offered a glimpse of the first bomber, still out at sea, and as the light swung, he saw a second, third, fourth and fifth behind. By the time the light had travelled a full turn, he believed he had counted eight enemy aircraft.

'Junkers,' Bomber gasped as he rejoined him. 'Ju eighty-eights. Twin-engined. Deadly. Eight of them, I think?'

Beau was too breathless to reply.

'Don't you worry. Our boys will know they're coming. Storm or no storm, they won't miss so many.'

Beau didn't know if this were true. But the only thing he had any power over was covering the ground between here and the road's end, and so that's where his priority remained, paws pounding beneath him.

'Keep going!' yelled Bomber. 'I'll chivvy Mabel along, best I can.'

Beau didn't turn to check. He thundered on, trying to avoid obstacles that veered up in front of him at the last minute. Sometimes he was successful, other times not. Yet he couldn't let them deter him.

He saw the bombers sporadically, looming larger in the lighthouse's beam and it angered him. How could they be

251

allowed to dance across the sea like this, bringing destruction and not caring whose lives they ruined? Where were the Air Force? Where were their own planes? How could they not be here when they were needed the most?

But just as his anger reached its peak there came another crack that wasn't thunder. He felt it in the ground upon which he ran. It was so ferocious that he sped up again, expecting the mud to open beneath him, sending him tumbling towards the gates of Hell. But the noise rolled up into the night sky. Beau still didn't know what it was, but the bombers did. He saw two, three, then four of them bank left then right steeply, disappearing from view.

'It's the Ack Acks,' shouted Bomber, above the din. 'Don't look back, keep going forwards.'

He did as instructed. 'Is Mabel with us?' he barked.

'I am,' came a voice. 'But I'm starting to regret listening to you, dog.'

There came a second crack, then more, too many to count in so short a time. Beau tried not to look but couldn't help it. He wanted to see some success: a direct hit, a mess of flames and burning metal careering from the sky, but there was nothing to be seen. Nothing except the reappearance of the bombers in the beam, one by one.

They were still coming. And it wouldn't be long now until they reached land.

52

Beau was not a newcomer to war, but that night he felt closer to it than ever before.

His ears rang with it, eyes stung with it, and he could smell its destruction with every single shell that was fired into the sky.

He could see the lighthouse's beam, so it wouldn't be long now until he spotted the houses next to it. How long then till the light in Peggy's window came into view, or better still, Peggy herself?

The only problem was that despite the frequency of their firing, the Ack Acks were having no success. Shell after shell pierced the rain, but not a single one reached its target. In fact with every one fired, the bombers seemed to grow in confidence, rolling left and right as if at some Sunday afternoon airshow.

'Why isn't it working, Bomber?' Beau barked. 'Why haven't they hit any planes?'

'Don't lose faith,' Bomber called back. 'Our boys won't let you down, and neither will I!'

And then it happened, as if on cue. A new noise, a new roar, followed by the most incredible sight – four planes appeared from nowhere, cutting left and right, fighting back the rain.

'Spitfires!' shouted Beau with delight.

'Hurricanes, actually, but the result will be the same, as soon as they find their range.'

The detail didn't bother Beau. All that mattered was that these planes held back the danger, or pushed it away from the lighthouse, away from Peggy. The Hurricanes wasted no time, eating up the space between themselves and the enemy, making themselves known, arranging themselves so they filled every inch of the Luftwaffe pilots' eyeline. But if the British planes were brave and true, then the Germans could match them for guile and skill, and so began the most terrifying of dances. The animals stopped momentarily to watch and saw a swarm of mini-battles, games of cat and mouse. Bullets ripped up the night, echoing over the bay, but for every bullet that was fired, there was a plane banking left and right, a steep incline that saw a plane's nose head straight for the heavens. It seemed to go on and on, this stalemate, until finally it happened – a blinding flash of white light followed by an orange ball of fire.

'Please tell me that was a German plane?' cried Beau.

'It was, it was!' Bomber replied, but the joy was short-lived, as high above them there was a second explosion that lit the entire sky, making the dimmed light from the lighthouse appear nothing more potent than a single struck match.

'Oh no, no, no, no, no, no,' wailed Bomber. 'That is not good, not good at all.' But no sooner had he spoken than there was another explosion to their left, and again, it was a British plane plummeting towards the sea.

This was not what was supposed to happen.

'Come on,' barked Beau. 'Let's keep moving. I've seen enough!'

The trio raced on with the sounds of battle still raging overhead. And then, oh, the most magnificent of sights, as there in front of them, was not just the lighthouse's beam, but the fuzzy shape of the building itself and the houses around it. This was no mirage, no trick of their tired, addled brains, they could see it, it was real.

It was not as tall as Beau'd imagined, more a squat telescope shape, with buildings on either side. But it was the single greatest sight Beau had ever seen. It was the only spur required. Nothing could stop him now. What was happening above was almost an irrelevance as long as he ate up the ground beneath him.

'Do you see it?' yelled Bomber above the incessant hammering of the machine gun fire.

'I do, we're nearly there, Bomber!'

'Just as I said,' cawed Bomber proudly. 'Don't stop. Keep going. And don't look back. You and Mabel will be there in minutes.'

His words didn't sound right. 'And you, Bomber. You too. Right beside us.'

But that's when Bomber did something unexpected. He landed in front of them, bringing them to a sudden stop.

'What are you doing?' Beau cried.

'The lighthouse is right there, you fool,' added Mabel.

'I always said I'd deliver you to it,' Bomber said, pride in his voice, but something else too. 'So now that I have, well, I'm needed elsewhere.'

He looked to the sky, where the two remaining Hurricanes dived and spun, trying to turn the most dogged defence into some kind of attack.

'Bomber,' Beau gasped. 'You aren't thinking . . . are you?'

Bomber looked incredulous. 'Well, of course I am.'

'Bird,' spat Mabel. 'I have listened to your delusions for months now, and largely, I've bitten my tongue. But if you are suggesting that you, a pigeon, are about to try and assist those planes against the rabid Luftwaffe, then you are a fool. A sad, deluded fool.'

They were strong words. But Bomber did not look offended. Instead he even chuckled, like he expected nothing less from the cat.

'Not a fool. Nor deluded,' he said simply. 'Just a soldier.'

'Please,' Beau begged him. 'Think about it, will you? For us? Think about how dangerous it is up there.'

'But I don't need to think. I know how dangerous it is. Just as we knew the same about our mission down here. We've dared to travel miles and miles. No food, no water or shelter. Think about what we've fought on the way and tell me that wasn't dangerous?' He cooed as if realising for the first time *exactly* what they had achieved. 'But we did it, didn't we?

We made it. So I need to go. Because the next mission, the one I was bred for, is right above our heads.'

Mabel hissed. 'Deluded,' she spat. 'Ridiculous.'

'You need to go,' Beau said.

'What?' Mabel clearly thought idiocy was now contagious.

'Bomber's right. He's a soldier. He got us this far and we can do the rest. Up there? Well, they clearly need him, don't they?'

'Thank you, friend,' said Bomber. 'I knew you'd understand.'

'Just make sure you get to the lighthouse as soon as you're done. I promised you a medal.'

'I'll look forward to it. Now run. Get to Peggy.'

But they couldn't. Not yet. They had to see their friend off. To wish him well.

So after a brief preflight check, Bomber threw himself into the night sky, heading straight into the fury above.

53

Beau and Mabel stood motionless, panting. Out of breath from the sprinting, of course, but also from the shock. They knew that they should be running, just as Bomber had told them to, but something was stopping them. To do so would be to abandon him, when every step of this journey had been completed as a trio.

'What do we do now?' Beau asked.

'Well, unless you're hiding some rather impressive wings under that matted fur of yours, I'd say there's very little we can do. And why did you gee him on like that?'

'It's called being a friend.'

'It's also called signing a death warrant, and if you want yours signing too, then standing here sounds like a pretty sensible thing to do.'

'We can't just leave him.'

'But the lighthouse is literally right there.' Mabel swallowed nervously, her own moment of truth perilously close now.

Beau had never felt conflict like it. He had been consumed by the thought of reaching Peggy for so long, but suddenly it felt like his paws were made of lead and his brain of jelly. He could not make the decision however hard he tried.

How typical it was then, that Bomber, despite not even

being with them, seemed to make the decision for them. There was a flurry of activity from above. The dogfight had been a one-sided affair, with the remaining Hurricanes engaged in a fierce rearguard action. But suddenly, from nowhere there came a change. How it happened, neither of them could pinpoint, but there must have been a distraction, or a lack of focus from the German pilot, as suddenly it was the machine guns of the Hurricanes that sounded, rattling the clouds. And it was one of the German bombers on the defensive.

'How on earth did that just happen?' gasped Mabel.

'I think we both know the answer to that,' smiled Beau. He had no doubt whatsoever, his tail wagging faster when the bullets found a home, deep in the German plane's engine, smoke pluming as it spluttered and then plummeted into the sea. 'Tell me that distraction wasn't Bomber's work!' he yelled, triumphant.

'It wasn't Bomber's work,' she said, deadpan.

But Beau disagreed, and watched agog as the Hurricanes carried on the offensive, bullying the Junkers, making them retreat into the clouds. But wherever they hid, they were found. It didn't matter that there were more of them, the British planes were galvanised, full of renewed hope, and within what felt like a minute, two more enemy planes were alight, spinning helplessly out to sea.

'He's doing it. He's doing it!'

'Unlike us, you fool. So unless you want us to have serious words for the millionth time, get moving. Now!'

Beau didn't move because she told him to. He ran because of Bomber. Because he knew that whatever was going on up there *was* down to his friend. He was there, causing havoc, doing whatever he had to, to forge a safe path for Beau. And if that was the case, then Beau had to grab the opportunity. His legs didn't like it, his lungs burned at the very thought of yet another dash, but they had no choice. This was it, the final sprint.

Above, the sky was on fire. Bullets zipped, shells cracked. The air seemed to be full of planes as they careered left and right, their throaty exertions never showing any sign of tiring. Bomber and co were definitely in the ascendency (whether Mabel believed it or not), and had zeroed in on a lone Junker, isolated from its squadron. The German pilot rocked left and right, making his plane as difficult a target as he possibly could, but with the Hurricanes closing in by the second, he did the most shocking thing. He released two of the plane's bombs, one falling without warning from beneath each wing.

Beau yelped in fear. 'What is it doing? What is it aiming at?'

'Maybe it's not aiming at anything?'

'What do you mean? That makes no sense!'

'I mean,' gasped Mabel without breaking stride, 'those bombs must weigh a tonne, slow them down. By dropping them, maybe it just gives him a chance of escape.'

But if this was the plan, then it proved to be fruitless, as the bombs falling turned out to be the Junker's final act. With magnificent accuracy, the Hurricanes' gunfire ripped at the tailfin, before peppering its rear, then wings. As the final bullet hit, making contact with one of its remaining bombs, the result made the world tilt and spin. The noise was deafening, surely heard back in London, whilst the sky was lit in such an angry orange blaze, it felt like the world was truly ending.

Beau and Mabel instinctively curled into balls as debris fell all around them. They had no control over any of it.

'Mabel!' Beau yelled, ears screaming after the Junker's final bombs hit the ground. 'Are you all right?'

'Wonderful,' the cat replied, sarcasm still intact.

'Can you see Bomber anywhere?'

'No, of course I can't. Stop asking ridiculous questions and run, will you.'

Mabel was off again, though visibly limping, and Beau felt a sense of panic as he raced past her: how could they be within spitting distance of their children, and yet still be in danger of not making it? So with a silent wish to Bomber to keep them safe for just a few minutes more, Beau began again, his body screaming its disapproval.

54

If this was war, then humans were welcome to it.

It was ear-shredding lunacy, pure and simple. Noise, catastrophe, fire and damnation. The sky burned, the land too, jagged pieces of aeroplane jutted randomly from the fields, or were sinking to the bottom of the sea.

Beau could feel the heat beneath his feet, had heard a number of further explosions, though how many, he couldn't be sure. They all seemed to be merging into each other.

He stopped a moment. His lungs were demanding it, which gave Mabel the time she needed to catch up.

'How does that lighthouse keep moving further away?'

'I was hoping you could tell me. I would ask Bomber, but he's still busy.'

He expected a snide response, but nothing came. The cat simply squinted into the night, counting the planes, working out herself that somehow, *somehow*, there were now two left on each side. Well, three for the Allies, if she allowed herself to include Bomber.

'Can we do this?' he asked her.

'Do we have a choice?' she gasped. 'Just don't tread on anything you shouldn't. I know how dim you dogs can be.'

Although he hated the sentiment, he did listen. The ground

was littered with tailfins and burning debris. With caution and stealth, the pets moved closer to their children and the lighthouse. The smell around them was changing too. Beau didn't know what it was filling his nostrils, but the smell was new yet familiar all at the same time.

'She's here!' he barked out to Mabel. 'Peggy, I can smell her!'

'Well, that's a relief,' gasped Mabel, but no sooner had she uttered the words, than the pair of them were blown clear off their feet. They felt and thought nothing, just tumbled and spun for what seemed like both a second and an age, as the sky became the ground and vice versa, over and over again.

They landed with a sickening thump, and Beau looked up at the stars, winded.

Only two planes remained, and if his eyes weren't tricking him, they seemed to be chasing each other along the coastline, moving further and further away.

The only other thing they could see was yet another ball of fire. And as Beau stared at it, he saw, very clearly, some twenty yards to its left, something small drop to the ground like a dead weight.

He was moving instantly.

He dashed through the amber rain, swearing he could feel his back smoulder and burn as the debris drizzled all around him. He was almost there, he was sure of it, and would not give up until he found exactly what had fallen.

He found it quickly. Too quickly. And the second he did, he wished that he hadn't.

As there, lying twisted on the floor, was his friend: feathers that always seemed so polished, parade-ready, now dull and lifeless, save for a small medal-sized cross of blood, that burned in the failing light. His wings were intact but lifeless, his eyes open, vacant, but looking in the direction that they had always looked: skywards.

'Bomber?' Beau cried. 'Oh, Bomber. Bomb!'

Nothing came back. Just the sound of his own heart thundering in his chest. He howled his name, again and again. Incredulous, heartbroken, but no matter how difficult the emotions were, the result did not change. The soldier was gone. Bomber was dead.

'Come away,' Mabel said, shocking Beau, who had no idea when she had arrived. 'You have to leave him. There's nothing you can do now.'

'But I can't,' Beau howled. 'I can't leave him.' He nudged him with his nose. 'Feel him. He's still warm.'

'That's as maybe, but he's still gone, dog. Even you know that.'

'I'm not leaving him. You go on.'

'I think we both know that won't be happening. In fact, *none* of this would be happening if it wasn't for this ridiculous bird.'

'And that's why I'm not leaving him.'

Mabel loomed over Beau, more panther than house cat. 'And you think that's what he'd want, do you? Do you think that bird navigated and motivated and led us all the way here, just for you to give up at the moment when you could finally have everything you wanted?'

'Everything I wanted?' Beau roared. 'You think I wanted this?' He pointed to his fallen friend. 'You think I wanted ANY of this?'

'Of course you didn't. But this is all we have. War just takes, blindly, leaving us to mop up whatever chaos it decides to leave behind. So the choice is yours, dog. We can come back for Bomber. We can. Give him the burial he deserves. But we can't do it now. Your girl is waiting for you, just over there. And my boy too.'

It would've have taken a lot to pull Beau away from his fallen friend. There were few words that could've moved him on. But hearing Mabel say that, telling him clearly that she needed Wilf too, was enough.

'And I can come back for him?' he asked. Just to be sure.

'As soon as you want. As long as you don't leave me behind.'

Beau straightened, heartbroken, and looked up.

The lighthouse's glare wasn't even in the distance now, it was above him, and he had to crane his head upwards to make sure he was definitely in the right place. As he checked one final time, he saw the last Hurricane fly victoriously above, banking sharply left as the pilot turned for home.

Beau howled, but felt little in the way of victory. It was a sorrowful noise, long and piercing, that saw Mabel recoil in shock. He cried again, then a third time, as long and loud as he

265

could muster, but as he breathed deeply to clear the way for a fourth, he heard a new noise: a loud creak, perhaps fifty yards away, but with that creak came the most seismic of changes, as his nostrils filled with something that even he had managed to forget.

Beau howled once more, the tone different this time: hopeful, pining, begging.

He heard the crunch of gravel, a pause ... then: 'Aunt Sylvie? Aunt Sylvie!'

There was a second voice, warning the child to stand back, to come inside, but the voice was redundant, ignored. The gravel sound came again, as did the smell, clearer and more precious than anything Beau had ever experienced in his life.

He pulled himself to his feet, exhausted, pained, but without care. As there she was. Taller than he had ever seen her. And despite the pain etched into her brow, more beautiful than he ever could've imagined.

He threw back his head and howled. The girl appeared to do the same.

'Beau?' she yelled. 'BEAU?'

She was rooted to the spot, not knowing whether to look forward or back. 'Aunt Sylvie, it's Beau. He's here!' She strained into the dark, eyes widening still further as Beau's companion edged beside him. 'And Mabel. Mabel too! Wilf. Come quick. Come quick!'

'Get inside, dear, for goodness' sake. It's not safe out there.'

'But it's Beau! And Mabel!'

'It can't be, sweetheart. They died in the bombing too. They must have.'

But Beau would never forget the sight of his girl, his Peggy, ignoring her aunt, pigtails bouncing as she tore across the grass, sweeping him effortlessly into her arms. As he flew skywards, he saw Mabel dash past too, as there in the doorway stood a bemused but ecstatic child, shouting his pet's name again and again.

Beau felt nothing but joy. He could smell nothing but his girl either, as he licked every part of her face. She pulled him so close to her that there was not an inch between them.

Beau hovered in her arms, weightless, careless. Fevered.

The road had ended. Not in the way that either of them had imagined.

But at the same time, a new road was beginning, and they would both be ready to walk it. Together.

The End

AFTERWORD

I never intended to write a series of novels set during the Blitz, so if you want to blame someone, well, it's all history's fault.

For every horrific tale of destruction and loss in those dark and awful days, there are also stories of unexpected valour and heart: the sort I seem incapable of walking away from.

Whilst Beau, Mabel and Bomber are fictional, there are several elements in *Until the Road Ends* which are real, or at least based on real people and events.

For a start, there *was* a dog like Beau, though he went by the name of Rip. Rip was a stray, found after heavy bombing in Poplar, East London, by an air raid warden. Adopted as a mascot, Rip proved himself to be the most remarkable of hounds, as despite no rescue training, he sniffed out over a hundred people still alive beneath the rubble of their homes.

It is said Rip's work persuaded the government to train other dogs in search and rescue, and he was awarded the Dickin Medal, the highest honour that can be bestowed on an animal, and the equivalent of the Victoria Cross. It was a medal that Rip wore proudly on his collar until the day he died. As soon as I read about Rip, I knew I had to write about him. He embodies so many qualities that I love in my own dogs.

The Balham underground station bomb that the animals encounter is also sadly rooted in fact. On the 14th October

1940, a 1,400 kg bomb detonated above the northern end of the platforms, where hundreds of people were sheltering. The underground station filled with water and earth, tragically killing over sixty people in the process. The photograph of the double decker bus half-submerged in a crater on Balham High Road has become a sad and recognisable image from the Blitz, representing the destruction it waged.

There are two other strands in the book which may feel a little far-fetched, but are both rooted in real life, the first being the cinema/dog sanctuary that our animal friends recuperate at. *How ridiculous,* you may scream. *As if?!*

But as it turns out there *was* a gentleman by the name of Bernard Woolley who turned his picture house into a dog rescue centre. The only difference was that the real Bernard lived in Lancashire, rather than in Bournemouth.

This brings us, finally, to the matter of Koringa and her wonderful crocodile Churchill. Whilst the idea of a croc on a lead drumming up ticket sales might sound ridiculous, history books tell us that it was a common occurrence in the 1940s, as Koringa toured the UK. In fact, she toured with five of the beasts, up and down the country. It was rumoured that Koringa also worked as a spy on behalf of the French Resistance. If ever a character deserved her own novel, it's her. Perhaps I might even try to write it, if another World War Two story doesn't get in the way first . . .

ACKNOWLEDGEMENTS

As always, I am in debt to many people, who helped and supported me in the writing of this book.

Professor Vanessa Toulmin for her invaluable insights into circuses and travelling shows, and for introducing me to Koringa.

Peter Saxton, who has long been a terrific friend and dim sum partner, but on this occasion steered me expertly when it came to trains.

Nigel Stoneman, who speedily and generously told me all about Sandbanks and the accompanying landmarks.

Jim Sells, who in the writing of all three World War Two novels has always been on hand to listen to my idiotic queries about the military – you're a lovely man and a true pal.

Thank you also to Sarah Crossan, Lesley Parr and Katya Balen, who never fail to keep me writing (or smiling), and I'd also like to mention August Sedgwick, who passed away while I was writing this book. August was one of the finest writers we had, for any age group, and I miss his friendship and love very much indeed.

Jodie Hodges continues to be the most brilliant agent and friend (thank you), and I'm so grateful to Emily, Molly and Jen at UA also.

My love and thanks to the wonders that are Andersen Press for their unwavering belief: Klaus, Mark, Chloe, Eloise,

Kate, Jack, Elen, Sarah, Rob, Liz, Sarah and Mary. To my PR partner in crime Paul Black, thank you for everything you continue to do (which is a LOT), and thank you to Charlie Sheppard, who has taught me what fun editing can actually be (who knew??). You're a wonder, you are.

Tom Clohosy Cole illustrated the beautiful cover to this book, and for that I will always be phenomenally grateful, as I will be to the booksellers, librarians and teachers who continue to push my stories so generously. Thank you.

Finally, I really couldn't do this without the support of my family, so cheers to Mum, Dad, Albie, Elsie, Stanley, Rufus, Bebe, Nancy and Lennie. And thank you to my wife, Louise (I won't ever get bored at marvelling how wonderful that sounds). I love you.

Hebden Bridge, December 2022

WHEN THE SKY FALLS

PHIL EARLE

1941. War is raging. And one angry boy has been sent to the city,
where bombers rule the skies. There, Joseph will live with Mrs F,
a gruff woman with no fondness for children. Her only loves
are the rundown zoo she owns and its mighty silverback gorilla,
Adonis. As the weeks pass, bonds deepen and secrets are revealed,
but if the bombers set Adonis rampaging free, will either of them
be able to end the life of the one thing they truly love?

'A magnificent story . . .
It deserves every prize going'
Philip Pullman

'An extraordinary story with
historical and family truth at
its heart, that tells us as much
about the present as the past.
Deeply felt, movingly written,
a remarkable achievement'
Michael Morpurgo

WHILE THE STORM RAGES

PHIL EARLE

September 1939. The world is on the brink of war. As his dad marches off to fight, Noah makes him a promise to keep their beloved family dog safe. When the government advises people to have their pets put down in readiness for the chaos of war, hundreds of thousands of people do as they are told. But not Noah. He's not that sort of boy. With his two friends in tow, he goes on the run, to save his dog and as many animals as he can. No matter what.

CUCKOO SUMMER

Jonathan Tulloch

Summer 1940. As the cuckoo sings out across the Lake District, life is about to change for ever for Tommy and his friend Sally, a mysterious evacuee girl. When they find a wounded enemy airman in the woods, Sally persuades Tommy not to report it and to keep the German hidden. This starts a chain of events that leads to the uncovering of secrets about Sally's past and a summer of adventure that neither of them will ever forget.

'A ripping wartime adventure and a love letter to Lakeland's farms and fells'
Melissa Harrison

Safiyyah's War

HIBA NOOR KHAN

War comes to the streets of Paris and Safiyyah's life changes for ever. Her best friend's family have fled, and the bombing makes her afraid to leave the mosque where she lives. But when her father is arrested by the Nazis for his secret Resistance work, it falls to Safiyyah to run the dangerous errands around the city. It's not long before hundreds of persecuted Jews seek sanctuary at the mosque. Can Safiyyah find the courage to enter the treacherous catacombs under Paris and lead the Jews to safety?

'*Safiyyah's War* has the soul of a classic & the urgency of a story for our times. A tale of tolerance, unthinkable bravery, and heart-in-mouth true events. I loved this book'
Kiran Millwood Hargrave

'All at once, *Safiyyah's War* broke my heart and filled me with immense hope. With its unforgettable characters and exquisite storytelling, this really is an extraordinary book'
A F Steadman

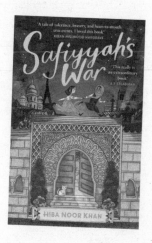

'Safiyyah is a protagonist I was rooting for all throughout; a lovely, kind-hearted girl whose story filled me in turns with despair and joy. This book shines through with kindness and empathy at its very heart'
Nizrana Farook

The Secret of Splint Hall

KATIE COTTON

1945. War has ended, but for sisters Isobel and Flora, the struggles continue. They've lost their father and had their home destroyed in a bombing raid, and now they must go to live with their aunt and her awful husband Mr Godfrey in their ancestral home, Splint Hall. From the moment of their arrival it seems that this is a place shrouded in mysteries and secrets. As the girls begin to unearth an ancient myth and family secret, the adventure of a lifetime begins.

THE BLACKTHORN BRANCH

ELEN CALDECOTT

NOMINATED FOR THE CARNEGIE MEDAL FOR WRITING

Cassie's older brother Byron has fallen in with the wrong crowd – it's soon clear these boys are wild, reckless and not human at all. They are tylwyth teg – Fair Folk, who tempt humans down into the dark places of the world. And Byron is tempted.

When he goes missing, Cassie and her cousin, Siân, follow his trail to an old abandoned railway tunnel which goes down and down into Annwn, the underworld. Here they find that the tylwyth teg are restless – and angry.

Their leader, Gwenhidw, wants to protect Annwn from the damage humans are doing to the world. Byron is part of her plan. But Cassie won't let her big brother be part of anyone's plan. Can she rescue him before it is too late?

'A story of magic, courage, redemption and recovery... a superb fantasy adventure' *LoveReading4Kids*

The MAGIC of ENDINGs

TOM AVERY

Jojo Locke's dad disappeared six years ago. And what's stranger still, none of his family can really remember him, there's a hole inside each of them where Dad should be. But then Aunt Pen arrives, a real faerie, with her tricks and wishes. She tests Jojo to see how deep his courage runs and sets him off on a journey to find their memories of Dad, and an adventure far beyond what he could have imagined begins.

'A resonant fantasy about how we commemorate those we have lost... [an] inventive, well-crafted novel'
The Sunday Times, Book of the Week

'Sparkles with magic'
Abi Elphinstone

'An intriguing mix of magic and adventure'
The Bookseller